SPOTS IN YOUR LOVE FEASTS

- JUDE 1:12 NKJV

A CONSUMING TALE of SINS THAT DEVOUR

REVISED EDITION (2024)

SPOTS IN YOUR LOVE FEASTS

A CONSUMING TALE of SINS THAT DEVOUR

REVISED EDITION (2024)

DAWN NICOLE EVANS

This book is a work of fiction. Although, all biblical scriptures referenced from the *Holy Bible* are true and noted from the *New King James Version*. All other characters, names, titles, programs, organizations and places are designed and depicted from the author's imagination or understanding of the *Holy Bible* and used or described in a fictitious manner. Any resemblance to actual persons, living or dead, or businesses or institutions active or inactive is purely coincidental.

Also note, while the author's depiction of hell is fictional, the place itself is very real and very active.

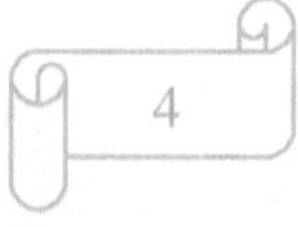

DEDICATIONS

First and always, thanksgiving to my Father God in heaven, who taught me with this work that compromise and compassion, are two very different things. Our Savior never compromised the truth to have compassion on us.

To my Dad, thank you for encouraging me, for being there for me, and your willingness to be one of my earliest reviewers.

To my Mom, who read to me as a child, growing in my heart a passion for storytelling.

To my church family, for being incredibly encouraging on this journey with me and making me feel that I have a part in something great.

"For there are many insubordinate, both idle talkers and deceivers, especially those of the circumcision, whose mouths must be stopped, who subvert whole households, teaching things which they ought not, for the sake of dishonest gain… To the pure all things are pure, but to those who are defiled and unbelieving nothing is pure; but even their mind and conscience are defiled. They profess to know God, but in works they deny Him, being abominable, disobedient, and disqualified for every good work."

– TITUS 1:10-11; 15-16 (NKJV)

A RESERVED PLACE

1

Maggie is pregnant! This is the first thing on my mind when I arrive at the restaurant, Maggie is pregnant and I forgot my watch in her bathroom. I set the expensive timepiece on the sink when I took a shower and after I got dressed, I remember reaching for it and knocking it into the little, pink waste bin at my feet, wedged between the cabinet under the sink and the base of the toilet. Like many meticulous young women, Maggie kept our little condo immaculately clean, especially the bathroom. Even that little, pink, plastic waste bin, which was so adorably feminine to me, was usually empty of any garbage when I came around for a visit. As I retrieved the watch from the bin, I saw the pregnancy test purposely buried, though not too deep, under discarded toilet paper, cotton balls and used floss. I knew Maggie was trying to say something to me, making known to me that she wanted a change, without saying so aloud, since that little pink bin never held even the slightest proof of Maggie's existence. When I came around there was never anything in that bin to indicate she was even human, with the normal, less pleasant bodily functions of a human. I recall setting the watch on the counter, quickly forgetting about it, as my attention was solely on the positive test amid the intentionally placed garbage. Maggie said nothing about it when I arrived and

I did not bring it up after I saw it. I left the test in the trash, believing she would do the mature thing and forget whatever else she was trying to achieve by leaving the test out for me to see in the first place. She would not burden me with this now, though the revelation still caught me off guard, which was why I left my watch behind.

By the time I arrive at the restaurant it is evening and a strange low hanging fog covers the street. The roads are slick and shiny as if it just rained though the sky was clear all morning. Without my watch, I do not know the exact time, but I am sure that I am late for this dinner meeting. I do not want to go into this with Maggie on my mind, or Linda or the kids, so I focus instead on the cuffs of my dark blue jacket and consider what I could have worn instead, maybe the jet-black suit with a powder blue dress shirt, or even a nice mint green just to seem easygoing? No, I should have worn the charcoal gray suit, a color that gives off a certain level of high regard and dominance, a look perfect for this meeting. Maybe after the interview I can find a tailor around here and get a few things made? For now, I would have to make do with the dark blue since it is already too late to return home and change. It is no surprise Linda picked this suit for me; most likely out of spite.

It still bothers me not knowing the time so I pat my pockets in search of my phone and realize I do not have that either. I remember setting the phone on Maggie's vanity in her bedroom before I went into the bathroom to take a shower. I could never leave my phone unattended around Linda, who was always in search of something to start an argument over instead of accepting things for what they are. Maggie on the other hand, knew all my secrets that she needed to know and I knew I could trust her or at least I thought I could trust her until I saw that test buried in the trash bin. Why had she not mentioned it? I suppose she thought I would get angry and I would have. In fact, I am a little angry about it now, well maybe angry is not the right word. More than anything, I think I feel frustrated. I have enough problems and Maggie was never one of them before today. Perhaps even frustrated is not the right word, I think I am really just disappointed in her. I knew Maggie to be careful and mature about many things, including our relationship. I never expected Maggie to try to trap me the way Linda did decades ago.

Since it would be pointless now to go back and retrieve my missing items or change my suit, I accept the fact that I will have to go into this interview unprepared. When he called me, Dr. Blight was professional enough to refer to tonight as a dinner meeting to assess my work but I was not going to let my guard down. I know Blight wants personal information about my past to see if I will be a good fit for this organization and considering my record, this will be a winning alliance for both of us. That is not to say I did not have indiscretions just as anyone else, but I refuse to let any of my past decisions hold me back from a successful future. Not all the time I spent running Eternal Affluence Church, which was severely limiting thanks to my father's lack of boldness and ingenuity, would be in vain. Collaborating with Dr. Blight now will give me the freedom to do all the things I had only imagined doing back in my old congregation.

I stand on the sidewalk directly beneath the streetlamp that pours over me like a spotlight, as I face the blacked-out window of the restaurant and study my own reflection. I look older and worn out, not a man in his late forties with better days ahead of him. My suit hangs a little loose as if it is now too big for me, even though it is tailor made. My face holds the suggestive signs of a sleepless night and my posture is terrible, as if I am carrying the whole world on my shoulders. Maybe that is why Maggie did not say anything aloud about the pregnancy test; even she could see how tired I am. With four kids already, three of them on the cusp of adulthood and still sponging off me like children, sometimes it is hard to manage. Did Maggie realize a new baby would be adding to my burdens? If she had thought about that beforehand, she would have taken better care of herself when we were together. When I saw that pregnancy test in her trash a wave of sadness did fall over me as I realized this would mean the end of our comfortable routine, it would mean the death of everything I enjoyed with her. The last thing I wanted was for Maggie to become another Linda and I did not want to do all over again what I'd done before with my first four kids, each one an utter failure to me.

I should have seen the changes in Maggie earlier. Her demeanor was subtly different, her usual bright smile and genuine joy seemed dimmer lately and slightly forced. Before I found the test, I just thought she was upset because I could not see her on her birthday and I promised her I would make it up to her another time. She knew when we first met that I had a very busy life outside of our little condo, with a wife, children and a church to run and that I was doing my very best to keep her comfortable and happy. Now I understand that maybe that was not enough for Maggie, wanting more than I have to give to the point of trying to force me into a corner. I swore after my marriage to Linda, that I would never let that happen again because now I know exactly where it will lead. As much as I like Maggie, I should have moved on a long time ago.

I stand up as straight as I can, trying to overcome my slouch while smoothing out my suit. I did not get to be lead pastor of one of the largest churches in the country by allowing others to manipulate me or force me to do what I did not want to do, to be what I did not want to be; I am nobody's puppet. Pushing aside the thoughts of Maggie and my family, I take a deep breath and enter the restaurant ready for the next stage of my life and career.

HORS D'OEUVRES or SOMETHING OUTSIDE of THE ORDINARY

2

I enter the dimly lit restaurant and scan the dining room. There are at least a dozen tables spread out across the floor closest to the front door, while a few more tables are peeking out from around the corner at the back. There are maybe ten to a dozen booths arranged along the wall surrounding the stand-alone tables, with each table decorated in black upholstered seating and soft white tablecloths. A single lit candle rests in the middle of each table and a wall sconce lines up with every other booth along the wall. The entire restaurant is basic and boring, in my opinion. As soon as I enter the room, the host is there to greet me with a forced smile. I do not react, but make him wait as I examine the room and search for Dr. Blight while smoothing out my suit self-consciously. The host seems to know who I am and whom I am meeting as he leaves his podium unattended to lead me further into the dining room without bothering to ask for my name. Even if I had been here before, I would not have remembered a place like this because it looked like a place easily forgotten by design. I follow the host to a booth seat against the wall where Dr. Blight is sitting with a glass of white wine set before him on the table. He does not look up when I approach.

"You're late. I was ready to leave about fifteen minutes ago." Blight says as he checks his gold watch in one smooth motion and I tug at my cuffs in envy and embarrassment. "Then I thought, no don't do that, give the family man a chance, a bit of a grace period. Perhaps he just got caught up in something?" Dr. Blight adds.

"My apologies Dr. Blight." I reply in my least apologetic tone. He is lucky that I showed up at all. "I can assure you, aside from tonight, I am always punctual." I explain and Blight pulls the corners of his mouth into an eerie smile as he motions for the host to leave us.

"Oh, I know, Mr. Graves, I'm only teasing, it's perfectly alright. I like this restaurant; it has a comforting ambiance to it that I would enjoy over a delayed meal any night. Now that you're here though, shall we order?" Blight suggests as I slide into the booth seat across from him. I nod in agreement but examine the room first instead. As far as ambiance goes, I suppose the doctor finds squinting his way through a gloomy dining area to be relaxing, because as far as I can tell the place does not have any modern electricity. A waiter appears with a tray of what looks to be some sort of turnovers and a fresh bottle of wine. I ignore the food and open my menu to find that I cannot read a single word. The writing is incredibly small and in some kind of fancy cursive font. I am familiar with fine dining but this is ridiculous! I attempt to lean in closer to the candle on our table to get a better look but I get too close and nearly catch the flame to the edge of my menu.

"Careful Graves, you don't want to burn the place down." Blight teases.

"Maybe setting the whole place on fire will give me enough light to read the menu?" I counter.

"You're not worried about cost are you? I told you this was my treat." Blight says with an insinuating tone and I scoff at the suggestion. Is he actually attempting to challenge my wallet? I want this partnership, but not at the cost of letting him think I *need* this partnership. A church is a church, and if necessary, I can go just about anywhere I want and fill the seats. Perhaps the doctor can see he offended me because he suddenly softens apologetically and offers assistance.

"Of course some of the signature dishes are printed a bit tiny aren't they? Well I know this is our first meeting in person, but would you be against my ordering for you? I have often dined here and I've tried nearly everything on the menu. I also think you and I share the same tastes, considering the fact that I also own a similar suit." Blight compliments my attire and I look down at my outfit with pride. The doctor's admiration for my charcoal gray suit helps me to relax a little. No need to get edgy with the man, I can be civil and friendly here, considering the fact that I did leave him waiting.

"Okay, why not, I guess I can trust you with my meal, Dr. Blight. If it's red meat, make it well done, and if it's chicken, make it baked." I explain confidently and Dr. Blight nods before motioning for the waiter. I sit back in the booth and pour myself a glass of wine, before remembering that it is white.

"I would expect a place like this to have a vintage Cabernet at least." I express in dissatisfaction. I learned years ago that it is best to voice your disappointment when it comes to service and selection but Dr. Blight just smiles, unfazed by my complaint.

"The white is the house specialty, bottled and stored at this very location. All of the ingredients are imported, but that only improves the flavor, and I can promise you it is delicious." Blight explains in promotion of the wine but I merely shrug.

"That's all well and good, but I'm still not a fan of white." I reply, though Blight's smile does not waver.

"At least give it a try." Blight suggests but I push the glass of wine a few inches away from me and reach for the turnover on the plate. I am not very hungry, but I am a fan of these. I pluck the pocket pastry off the tray and find it still warm and slightly crispy on the outside. I bite into the bread and while the texture is most likely ground beef with some sort of cheese, the taste is completely absent. I chew slowly and thoroughly, but I can get no flavor whatsoever. Even Linda could have done a better job on these. I swallow the first bite of food, finish the rest of the bland turnover quickly, and decline another. Blight stuffs an entire turnover into his mouth, licks his fingers and looks at me questioningly.

"You don't like the hors d' oeuvres?" He asks.

"They're bland." I reply, slightly surprised to be in such a nice restaurant that serves such terrible food. Blight does not seem to notice the lack of taste in the food. He shrugs and takes the rest of the tray with the remaining four turnovers for himself.

What sort of doctor is he anyway? I look away, not wanting to see him devour his food like a starving animal, and my eyes fall on my discarded glass of wine. The liquid looks cloudy at first, sort of murky and I turn the glass by its stem to get a better look but as I turn the glass I realize it is just a trick of the light or lack thereof. Blight's promotion of the wine stirs me to give it a chance. I take a small sip and find it very refreshing and sweet. With each taste, the flavor becomes more and more overwhelming. I finish the glass and begin to pour myself another when I realize Blight is watching me.

"It's good isn't it?" Blight asks with a grin.

"Very good, I guess I misjudged white wine all this time." I concede as I finish off another glass. At least something in this restaurant is worth the trip. As I drink, I look around the room to check out my fellow diners and see the dining room is not too crowded yet. I do not mind this at all, as sometimes I like things quiet and private. In fact, there is so much space between our table and the next occupied table that I cannot hear anyone else's conversation. When Dr. Blight asked me to meet him here, I figured he heard I was reigniting my pastoral career and he wanted to bring me into his organization, being well aware of my work, from what he claimed. After the call I considered what I would say when he asked what caused me to leave Eternal

Affluence in the first place. I had not settled on a response yet to best phrase my ousting.

"Well, while we wait for our appetizers, how about we catch up on a few things? I'm not one to begin on a sorrowful subject, but I must offer my condolences on the death of your mother." Blight says as I take another drink and find a slightly bitter aftertaste, almost unnoticeable, but I am sure it is there and just as quickly, it disappears. I consider why Dr. Blight would bring up such an old issue, as my mother died years ago, but I merely smile politely and allow Blight to continue. "Miss Adelaide's life proved to be quite the redemption story with an … unexpected ending, you might say." Blight adds as I refill my glass.

"I guess so and I appreciate your condolences but I wasn't even aware you knew my mother." I reply.

"Oh, yes, I'd been following her influence for quite some time, as well as your father's." Blight replies and I scoff.

"My mother didn't have much in the way of influence for you to follow. When my dad was alive, she was his shadow and after his death, she was his echo. I don't think she ever really did anything of her own will or opinion." I reply bitterly, recalling how my mother kept to my father's wishes for his replacement of lead pastor of the church he led for nearly thirty years.

"You sound a bit disgruntled about that." Blight suggests and I shake my head quickly.

"Oh no, I have nothing but love for my mother and I forgave her for our strained relationship. Like my father, she had no faith in me and really none in herself, which is why I pitied her a little. In fact, after my father died, I was more than happy to take care of her while succeeding Dad in running the church." I add quickly to cover my anger over those old memories and Blight looks at me curiously.

"But you didn't succeed him, did you?" Blight asks and I frown but hide it quickly under a drink from my glass. The wine is getting its flavor back. I examine the bottle, but the name seems to be in a foreign language with exaggerated cursive script similar to the menu, making it difficult to read.

"No, I didn't run the church in my father's place, at least not immediately." I admit and Blight waves his finger in the air as if bringing to remembrance what I want to forget.

"That's right, you were passed over for the job and that young man that went to school with you was promoted to lead pastor. What was his name again?" Blight asks in a way that tells me he already knows the answer.

"Miles Abbott, and yes, he was promoted to lead pastor, but no, I was not *passed over*, the senior board took a vote and felt that Miles was a better fit at the time. Most likely because he was not raising a family as I was and could dedicate more time to the church then I could." I explain as I refill my glass and feel the weight of the bottle growing light. I motion to Blight, who motions to the waiter, who appears immediately to replace the bottle. We raise our glasses to one another in a toast as Blight continues.

"Your mother was on that board, it's a little strange that she didn't vote for you." Blight says and I feel the anger rising inside of me all over again. I knew it! Mother claimed she made the best choice she could, without answering me directly as to whether or not she pushed for my placement into Dad's former position, and now I am positive that she did not even vote for me. She was heartless, selfish, and never believed in me. Before replying, I inhale deeply to calm myself down.

"Whether she voted for me or not, it would've been one vote out of five. Either way they chose Miles and they had a good run with him for three years. During that time, I had a comfortable position as overseer of the youth program. That gave me an opportunity to downsize my responsibilities when my twins reached college age, which then gave me more time to dedicate to the church when I was finally appointed lead pastor." I explain.

"And this was after your mother's stroke, correct?" Blight asks. I smile over the memory of my mother's helpless, frail body.

"Oh, yes, the poor thing, she could barely speak and she was in constant discomfort and struggle. I suppose that was the most comforting about her death, she was finally at peace and went home to be with my father and our heavenly Father." I reply, though somehow I doubt my mother had gone where she expected in the afterlife. Dr. Blight laughs quietly.

"What's so funny?" I ask.

"Oh, nothing, I was just considering what you said about home going. I always thought that to be unintentionally accurate phrasing for every death. Why else would one not just say the deceased went to heaven? Especially when the term home going makes one wonder exactly to which *home* the deceased individual has gone to, the intended home made for them or the one they erroneously made for themselves. I mean, don't get me wrong, I'm sure a woman like your mother is in that paradise she so yearned for at the end of her life, but what of the others?" Blight asks and I stare at him, confused.

"What others?" I ask and Dr. Blight waves his hand gently in the air as if to conjure up something floating there.

"The others, people, I mean." Blight replies before leaning in close across the table. "Can we talk? I mean *really* talk. I don't like having these coded conversations with pastors and ministers. You know the sort, when they say what they think they *should* say but not what they really *want* to say. You understand?" Blight asks in barely above a whisper and I raise an eyebrow in doubt. Was this a test? Was Blight trying to back me into a corner so he could interrupt my comeback? As if reading my thoughts, Blight explains himself further.

"This isn't some sort of trick. I know your history Graves. I know what caused you to leave your previous church and the scandals surrounding everything. That's why we're here, right now, tonight in this quiet and exclusive restaurant so that you and I can speak candidly to one another. Your story is for me and me alone. There is no press here, no cameras here and no judgmental disbelievers screaming for a review of your bank statements. All I ask is for your genuine honesty. I mean it must be incredibly overwhelming to keep all that inside." Blight adds and I sit back heavy with unease. Blight already knew about my departure from the church. I came here thinking I could at least explain my side of the story. That this could be my shot at a comeback and there was no reason it could not be. Blight himself just admitted that all he wanted was the truth, and I was the only person who could give it to him. I empty my glass and savor the flavor, as this fresh bottle of wine is sweeter than the first.

"Alright Dr. Blight, what would you like to know?" I ask with all the bravado I can muster. I will wear my past with pride. I made my decisions with the best intentions and I have no regrets. Blight brings his hands together joyously in a small clap and smiles just as our appetizers arrive. The waiter removes the empty dishes that once held the turnovers, which Blight finished completely, then sets a large tureen and a tray of rolls in the center of the table.

"Splendid!" Blight cheers and we begin our meal.

APPETIZERS or SOMETHING TO TEASE THE APPETITE

3

"You don't know how glad I am that you'll open up to me. I want people in my inner circle to trust me and know that they can share anything with me." Blight explains as he uses a large ceramic ladle to distribute some soup out of the tureen and into two small white bowls. He then uses a set of tongs to pluck two large rolls from the tray, placing them onto small white plates with delicacy as he is talking. "So, let us begin with something basic like what I spoke of a moment ago about home goings and death in general. I can't help but wonder, what does a pastor such as you think best to do or say when it comes to explaining hell?" Blight asks as I draw the dish to myself and dip my spoon into the thick soup; it is hot but Blight does not hesitate to finish off his first bowl quickly.

"Well, hell is easy enough to handle, fire and brimstone don't need much explanation." I reply as Blight is chewing the bread delicately and savoring every part of the dish. He closes his eyes as I am talking and I am unsure if he hears me at all until he begins to shake his head and wag his finger in the air again.

"No, no that's not what I mean at all. What I want to know is, how would you, as a pastor explain to a person who has just lost a loved one, about the afterlife? As a pastor, how do you explain if the departed has gone to heaven or hell?" Dr. Blight asks. The question catches me completely off guard and I wonder what sort of assessment this is? Blight takes another spoonful of soup as I consider my answer.

"Well, that's easy too; I suppose I just don't say anything about it at all. At least I would never tell a member of my congregation or anyone else that their loved one might have gone to *hell*. No one wants to hear something like that." I reply and Blight nods in understanding as I take another drink.

"Of course, but I've learned over time that when it comes to death and judgment, all sorts of questions come to mind in an individual and I find it unusual that no one has ever asked you such a question about a dead loved one." Blight continues.

"You're surprised no one has ever asked me that? Why would someone ask *anyone* a question like that at all?" I counter in frustration.

"For closure of course." Blight replies calmly.

"Well, how in the world would I know whether a member of my congregation went to hell or not?" I ask and Blight shrugs.

"You're a pastor, you should understand by now the keys to heaven and hell." Blight replies and I flush with embarrassment.

"Of course I understand heaven and hell. I just mean … I mean I know what it takes for a person to go to heaven and what gets a person sent to hell." I add defensively and Blight looks surprised.

"Do you? Well that's good to know." Blight replies and I detect a slight amount of sarcasm.

"Yes I do. What I mean is why would someone ask me specifically? I don't know what anyone else does in private. A person could be committing all sorts of sins at home behind closed doors while outside they could be the kindest person I've ever met." I explain and Blight smiles.

"Funny thing about sins, some of them have a way of beginning in secret but they don't stay that way. Then again, I understand your point, humans can only really see what is on the outside, not the inside, but that doesn't mean you can't know a person by their works and those who sow evil cannot hide the reaping of it. So let's focus on the more obvious transgressors, the type that don't mind when the whole world can see their monstrous side. Take a murderer or rapist perhaps; in fact, let's use that as an example." Blight suggests as he refills his bowl from the tureen. I take the pause to try a spoonful of my own soup, and like the turnovers, it is bland and flavorless. I reach for the seasoning in the center of the table as Blight begins eating again, forgetting all about his question for the moment.

"What kind of soup is this?" I ask Blight, who raises his hand to silence me. He swallows slowly then looks at me.

"It is the house soup, a signature dish and perfectly crafted. Now, where were we? Oh, yes, of course an example. Let us play make believe for a moment. Let us *pretend* that you are you and I am a young man of your congregation whose brother has just died but not in any ordinary fashion. Let us say, my brother was a notorious fiend who killed nearly a dozen people and after his capture, he admitted to his crimes, showing nothing but pride for his misdeeds. Let us also say he had no remorse for the suffering he brought to his victims and their families and was quite open and unapologetic about what he'd done. Let us say my brother held all the character flaws humanity identifies with pure evil, or more accurately, he held all the characteristics of a corrupted spirit according to the Word of God. Then that fateful day arrives and the governing authorities take his life in retribution for the lives my brother had taken. Now when it is all over, I approach you and ask, 'Is my brother in hell?' What would you tell me?" Dr. Blight asks and I realize this is the most unorthodox interview I have ever had. I set the seasoning down and try the soup again, but still no taste. It is just … flavorless cream. I push the bowl to the side and refill my wine glass, taking a drink as I consider Blight's scenario. He wants me to be honest, but in my profession, honesty is like walking on thin ice. It could be the death of a pastor's career to speak the truth.

"Well, I suppose I would find it best to …" I begin but Blight interrupts me, wagging his finger again, this time directly in my face and I'm about ready to cut the offending digit off. Blight finishes his second bowl and empties the rest of the tureen for a third helping. I sit back in the seat silently nibbling on the bread, which is also bland and flavorless. I have always hated these flamboyant types.

"I don't want to hear what you *suppose*, or what you'd find best to say. I want *your* truth as best you can give it." Blight explains. This is ridiculous. I run my fingers through my hair and exhale. I can give him the truth but first, another drink.

"Okay, I would tell him, *you*, I would tell *you* that your brother is rotting in hell. If I were honest, I would say to you that your brother was a low-life waste of oxygen that was writhing and burning in the pits of agony at that very moment. I would tell you that if anything worse than hell could happen to an individual, I would hope it happened to him. How is that for truth?" I reply sharply but Blight merely shrugs as he is unmoved by my hostility and aggressive opinion.

"Well, I suppose that's the best response I'll get for a hypothetical question. I must ask though, why wouldn't you just be this honest in the first place if someone asked about their loved one going to heaven or hell? Why couldn't you just tell them what you really thought?" Blight asks.

"I already told you, I wouldn't know whether they went to heaven or hell. Not every case of life, death and judgment is so black and white. There is a gray area to sin and just because someone admits to a crime does not mean they actually did it and if they did, maybe they had a reason, so I can't even base my judgment off of a trial and a jury. Either way, in the end there is always forgiveness. I get that funerals can be cheesy and overly dramatic especially when a person wants desperately to believe that a loved one is in heaven; but I don't believe every funeral is filled with exaggerations of the dead and their deeds, there are good people in this world and God sees the heart. Even with bad people, sometimes a person needs to exaggerate in a eulogy because not everyone can be open and honest about the dead. It's all about honor and esteem, not everyone wants to leave someone with a tarnished reputation. Maybe it's a subtle fear that the same thing will happen to them when their time comes? Someone will bring to light all their lurid indiscretions and mistakes and the dead can't be there to defend their choices or at least have an opportunity to explain. Then there is the case of who is to judge whether those indiscretions or mistakes are enough to make a person hell-bound." I explain as Blight finishes his soup and a waiter's assistant appears to remove the empty dishes. The assistant reaches for the remains of my soup, but Blight rests his fingers on the lip of the bowl and looks at me.

"Were you going to finish that?" Blight asks and I shake my head and take another drink of wine. Blight waves the assistant away while claiming my partially eaten dish for himself with an eager grin.

"It's best eaten when it's burning hot, but it's quite good cooled as well." Blight explains as he is practically salivating over my discarded food and I have to look away in disgust. He actually has no problem with eating the remains of my meal like a raccoon or something.

"You know I never said you had to base a person's guilt off of a trial and jury; as no human being can truly know another's guilt or innocence in every matter, which is why it's so easy to judge on speculations and rumors. The root of things like intention and heart are not so clear in the natural world. I was only asking how you would handle such a situation if someone came to you seeking answers and peace of mind. I'd like your opinion on very clear and obvious actions and lifestyles of individuals, but if it is as *you* say, then the majority of the population actually believes their eternity rests on what other people say and think of them, what a pathetic notion. Whatever the cause for such worries or concerns, all the funerals I've attended were sullied and burdened with false or desperately embellished exploits, flat humor, fictional stories of kind or unselfish acts and biblical quotes which the departed themselves never quoted and more so never applied in lifestyle. According to you, what matters most to the living is what people think of them when they are dead. If all the people I've encountered who claim to believe in judgment and follow *His* word, had any kind of true faith, wouldn't they make a greater effort to live the lifestyles *He* commands instead, and go to that good place? Though if that were to be done, we'd see a lot less of those who have eulogies of a good life never lived and just end up going to hell anyway." Dr. Blight explains candidly. His unusual view of the world is appalling.

I have never met anyone who openly discussed people this way. It was a little refreshing actually to hear some unfiltered truth.

"Actually I don't know if people care about what others think of them and I don't know how many people are lying about their lives, which is exactly why I give the same sermon at every funeral. It's offensive to just assume someone went to hell when they died." I reply a little sharply and Blight opens his mouth in a silent, understanding "Oh" and nods his head.

"Offense, of course, it's always about offense." Blight mumbles to himself and I take another drink while trying to figure out what I have gotten myself in to.

"Why would you ask such a strange question anyway? What does heaven and hell have to do with my past work?" I ask and Blight sits back in his seat before motioning for another bottle of wine. I had not noticed that we finished off the last one.

"Well, it isn't a question about *your* past work or a qualification so much as it is a question about a survivor's mind and weaknesses. You see, in our line of work it is best to focus not on what was lost in death but on what we can still gain among the living. There is always a chance of missing vital opportunities in funeral ceremonies to seek out weak points in the surviving family members. For a believer, death is tricky to explain. Some misunderstand the afterlife, making one think that a life of sin might not always lead to an eternity of torment. As if God would suddenly change *His* Word for specific individuals who willingly turned away at every opportunity while making no effort to change and being completely unapologetic for their sinful actions. Some actually believe *He* might just decide to accommodate everyone who never acknowledged *Him* at all in life and bless the sinner along with the faithful with eternity in paradise anyway. I only wanted to know how you, as a pastor tell someone in mourning that there is a chance the person they'd just lost had gone to hell, perhaps to inspire the living to avoid the same mistakes." Dr. Blight explains.

"The truth or what could be the truth, is the last thing a person in mourning wants to hear. No one wants to consider where their sins might get them when they die, because it can take the joy out of living." I explain as I consider the few sermons I spoke on the subject of death. I learned early on in my career that it is better to speak of the pleasures of life rather than the convictions.

"Of course, to live like you don't know there are consequences for tomorrow is the greatest gamble." Blight replies with a smile.

"Well, then you understand my point in using comforting sermons. I mean, I suppose funerals could be used to preach a message of kindness or even to suggest that individuals get to church more often, but that sort of thing doesn't sit well with everyone. I don't think anyone really wants to hear that what they might be doing in their lives is wrong." I explain further and Dr. Blight nods in agreement giving me a bit of encouragement. Maybe there was something to this honesty path?

"Another problem with humanity in dealing with grief is the struggle to understand how the Savior could conquer the grave but people keep dying. For the seasoned believer it's more about holding on in prayer and faith only to lose anyway and wonder what went wrong, or even how to explain their faith after God has seemingly taken someone from them. Therefore, as the individual questions death, this leads to the questioning of God and *His* word, which then leads to questioning if *He* is still there or ever was in the first place. In such cases, there is an abundant selection to administering a downfall. So many opportunities for spiritual corruption by planting further confusion, misdirection and fear to create conflict with everything an individual may believe about their Creator as holding any truth. I've seen firsthand how death can be a faith-breaking tool among humanity, when mixed with a large dose of pride, of course." Blight explains.

I pour another glass of wine while he carries on. How many have I had so far? I am not one for overindulging in alcohol, but there is nothing else for me here in the way of food. The main course would arrive soon and I am losing hope it will have any flavor at all.

"What do you mean about mixing pride with confusion?" I ask, just barely registering what Blight said.

"Well, when a person can't explain something, they usually disregard it altogether instead of admitting any fault in their own understanding. It is the human way to blame the question for being so complicated, as it is easier than the humility of asking for help with the answer. The same is often done with the *Manual*, when some people cannot understand it, instead of seeking the right spiritual guidance from *He* who inspired it, they find the wrong teachers to give them a depiction of it. This flawed interpretation leads one to question the entire validity of the *Manual* itself and *He* who inspired it." Blight explains and I nod, not wanting to admit I do not understand what he is saying.

"Do you always talk like this?" I ask and Blight looks up in surprise.

"Like what?" He asks.

"In riddles sort of; you sound like that monster from a Greek tragedy I read in high school, or a character from one of those children's books with the made up words and strange characters." I explain loosely, unable to recall the names of either and Blight burst into laughter, throwing his head so far back I can see his unusually sharp looking canines.

"That's funny, I like that. I suppose my speech is rather strange; not so much like the Sphinx of the great tragic trilogy, but possibly more like *Him* with all *His* parables. I always thought my studies made me very theoretical in my language, while my work is successful execution of those theories. I've spent my whole existence studying the *Manual* just to do the work I do so it's no wonder it has had some effect on me." Blight explains with a strange expression of bitterness as if recalling a bad memory.

"The Manual?" I ask, just as two bowls of another type of soup arrive, though this one has more meat than liquid in it, so it is more like a light stew. Blight shuts his eyes in an expression of ecstasy as he deeply inhales the aroma of the dish. I sniff the bowl and it does smell delicious, but I will not go off aroma. Blight and I dip our spoons in at the same time and he is savoring the same flavor I am still searching for as I hold the stew in my mouth. It is hot but like everything else I have tried so far, there is no real taste. What is going on? I scowl at Blight who is obviously exaggerating the flavor. I hope he has room in his stomach for my bowl too. After he takes a few more bites, Blight quickly brushes off my inquiring of his Manual.

"You know what I mean. It's the *Manual* for us, a study guide of the trade." Blight explains briefly and I still have no idea what he is talking about, but I let it go. Blight returns his attention to the stew, chewing loudly and with nothing else to do, I decide to try my bowl again. I take another spoonful, this time with a bit of what looks like steak and begin to chew slowly but still I get absolutely nothing. How in the world was this even possible?

I examine the rest of the stew, which looks completely fine, but I am not going to waste any more time on it. My glass is empty so I take the fresh wine bottle directly to my lips to get some kind of taste out of this dinner. Blight gets a good laugh at my wild behavior and I feel like a fool. I have never done anything like that before as I have always had an image to maintain. I do not consume alcohol often but I know how to drink wine properly, like an adult and not a drunk.

"Don't be embarrassed. The food is an acquired taste." Blight offers while still laughing at me.

"Acquired taste nothing, this stuff is flavorless! Whoever cooked this food has no business near a toaster much less in a kitchen." I exclaim while still disgusted over the bland taste of the meat, which adheres to my tongue. My complaint surprises Blight who leans over his own bowl as if to examine the food more closely. He shrugs and continues eating.

"You should never say things like that as it's an insult to the cook. The last person you want to offend is the one handling your food. You don't like it, just say so and leave it at that, but to complain about his style is just rude." Blight tries to correct me but I frown and push my bowl across the table to him as he welcomes the extra dish. "Well, now that we're on the finale of the appetizers, I suppose we should get on with the assessment. Remember, we are still on our little honesty agreement, correct?" Blight reminds me and I raise the entire bottle of wine in the air in salute.

Anything that would get me out of this restaurant, I was open to and this collaboration had better be worth my time. As Blight adds the same seasoning I used previously on the soup, to his bowl of stew, I look around the room again to see that business is beginning to pick up. More diners now occupy half the tables, which seems normal except for the fact that each occupied table has only two diners, just like our own. Even the tables with four sides and room for four chairs only have two seats and two people there. I figure perhaps it is some strange policy of the restaurant and look away disinterested and pour myself another glass of wine.

"Well, before we get into the specifics of the assessment, I forgot to ask, how is your family? Your wife and children, you have four offspring, correct?" Blight asks and I feel uneasy over how much he knows about me. Though his knowledge of my professional and personal life is not unusual considering how much time I spent in the public eye during and after my time running Eternal Affluence. My wife and kids were in the spotlight just as much as I was. In fact, Linda seemed more upset about how she and the kids felt the pressure of a microscope on everything they did, than she was over my own indiscretions. As if my family's actions did not reflect on my career in the same way.

"They're doing very well actually; my eldest children, the twins Jay and Sasha, just finished college together, both with honors. Jay has gotten married while Sasha is seeing someone as well. My youngest son Braden is so into his tech I hardly understand what he's saying anymore, but if it makes him the next billionaire mogul, I don't mind." I explain with forced humor and Dr. Blight pauses over his stew to study me. He looks confused, as if he can see right through my embellishments. He licks his lips slowly, most likely considering what I have said, but to my relief, he does not question any further.

"And Ramona, she's your youngest daughter correct? How is she?" Blight asks. Is it just my imagination or is there a twinge of saltiness in his tone when he mentions Ramona?

"She's well now, considering that she took mother's death really hard. Ramona cared for my mother after her stroke when she moved in with us. I thought she would have a great future in nursing back then, Ramona I mean." I reply.

"So she spent a great deal of time with her grandmother, yes?" Blight asks absently.

"Well, yeah, like I said Ramona took good care of her grandmother when she fell ill and became a great nurse for my mother." I repeat.

"I'm sure it was more than just average nursing. Your mother Adelaide was an unexpected influence when it came to faith. She and your daughter Ramona spent a great deal of time in prayer and worship together, studying and learning things beyond your teachings." Blight adds and I frown.

"Well I don't know what they could've learned beyond my teachings but I suppose they spent time singing and praying together. I don't really know for sure as I wasn't able to spend very much time with my mother before her death. I was still adjusting to my new position as lead pastor." I reply, turning the conversation back on to more important matters.

"That's right; you did eventually achieve your coveted promotion *after* your mother fell ill." Blight adds and I give him a sharp look. I did not appreciate his emphasis on when I was promoted, but I would not have to say so just now. "Remind me exactly, as to how that came to pass." Blight adds and I sip my wine while trying to recall the story exactly as I told it in the past.

"Well, some of Abbott's methods came under scrutiny, and it was decided that he and the church should part ways." I reply. Blight runs his fingers through the stew bowl, licking up every drop of the contents as I talk. I pull a face but try not to let him notice. For a doctor and perhaps my future business partner, he is incredibly savage. Blight pulls his fingers from his mouth and begins to shake his head.

"Now, now, Mr. Graves, we had an agreement to honesty, remember?" He reminds me and I frown.

"I was being honest. I am being honest. Abbott moved on to a better fit for himself and I was appointed lead pastor." I reply with a straight face. Blight could not possibly know the difference.

"So if you're telling the truth; my file is incorrect and you didn't plant seeds of division within the church to … overthrow your competition?" Blight asks with a sly grin. The look of guilt on my face is apparent enough to make Blight smile wide but he says nothing more. How could he have guessed that? I exhale and set my wineglass down on the table. Well, what is the point of hiding the true story now?

"Why is any of that important to you? What matters is that I was running the church, finally, as I should have been years earlier. It doesn't matter how

I got there, the point is that I got there." I explain and Blight nods as the assistant returns to collect our dishes.

"I like that, I like that very much. Forgoing the words of chapter MW7:13-14 of the *Manual* to live as if the narrow gate is unimportant altogether; it is ultimately the final destination that is paramount." Blight replies and I nod uneasily. I did not like how comfortable he was getting with me and what was the Manual he kept referencing? This whole evening is feeling strange to me. I am the one who is used to bringing a certain amount of intensity to a conversation that would make anyone I was talking to become very adamant in pleasing *me*. As if it is the most important thing for a follower to find favor with the man that represented their Savior. Perhaps that is what drew Maggie to me?

"But as much as I like you Mr. Graves," Blight continues, "I find myself disheartened by your lack of trust. We agreed to an honest conversation and without one I cannot gain anything from you that I don't already have." Blight explains. I refill my glass and look Blight straight in the eye. Is he turning me down for a partnership now because he thinks I am lying? What does it matter, if it is all between us? I want this partnership and I know I deserve this position. As if reading my mind, Blight speaks up again.

"I need to know what type of man you are. A man who will do anything to get to where he knows he belongs, or a man who waits for convenience to open the door? Of course people who wait for convenience always seem like cowards to me, as if they needed an exterior excuse to make up for their lack of boldness. Are you bold, Mr. Graves? Or are you a coward?" Blight asks as he sniffs the wine casually from his glass but does not drink. I can feel the burn rising in my neck and cheeks.

"I guided the kids; the ones who spoke out against Abbott, claiming he was inappropriate in his conversations with them. He was so meticulous about his contact with people, physically, and on a lesser level, verbally. I saw an opening and I used it to my advantage. I spent time with some of the youth closest to him and a few of the kids that detailed getting legitimate, proper advice from him about growing up and their struggles. When some kids would talk to me, I would suggest things; like, maybe a harmless comment made by Abbott to them, was not so harmless. Eventually a few of the teens got together and complained to the senior committee. I was a little worried they would mention my name, but they didn't, and I realized that I had a knack for planting doubt and creating controversy. Before I persuaded the teens to complain, I started rumors among the congregation as to how Abbott could afford such a nice house and a nice car and all those suits he'd wear when he was teaching." I admit to Dr. Blight. He begins to chuckle and I smile back as we raise our glasses to one another in a toast.

"Now that is what I want to hear. I'll bet it was quite fun planting seeds like that; to exaggerate the house, the car, and even the suits. You know he only had three of those, no name brands, just nice and properly made that he wore in rotation only on Sunday when he was teaching, simply because he was used to it. It's amazing the division one can create when character or finance is brought into the conversation. I've seen people get offended at the sight of the offering basket. They leave the church, vowing never to come back because, 'All that church cares about is money!' Incredible what the removal of one word can do to a whole culture." Blight says thoughtfully.

"What do you mean? What one word?" I ask and Blight pulls his brows together as if trying to remember.

"I believe it is in chapter 1TY6:10 of the *Manual*, 'The love of money being the root of all kinds of evil.' You see, those words are very true, as to *love* money or chase it or do anything to gain more and more of it for the sole purpose of having more and more of it can be a road to greed, malice, murder, hate, immorality, and every other sin one can think of. It all usually comes back down to the *love* of money. However, when you remove the word *love*, you have an opportunity to make wealth itself into something evil. To *have* money becomes the root of all evil, no matter how you use it or how it is gained. For example, a pastor that has a nice house in which to house themselves and their family, or a car to get to and from work is condemned for his or her increase and blessings. Though it may or may not be God-given, all is lumped together in a worldly analysis that the teacher of God's Word does so for profit and profit alone. Amazing how often people overlook the provision in the *Manual,* spoken of and given by their God, and yet they believe their struggle to make ends meet or their lack in all things to be the deciding measurement of their righteousness. Poor souls, if only they knew that times of lack were to glorify the abundance of their God and the times of God-given abundance can reveal what is lacking in the world. With this Scriptural misunderstanding or misquoting, you can make a believer feel guilty because they have a bed to sleep in; or guide a believer to judge another for having a nice pair of shoes. Guilt and jealousy are easier emotions to work with than gratitude especially when it comes to provision." Blight explains as he holds his wine glass in the air thoughtfully.

I can only stare at him completely appalled by what I am hearing. This one is an odd sort, but strangely enough, I find myself drawn to what he is saying. It is true that I planted rumors of Abbott's greed and even went so far as to get the senior counsel to check the financial records for any suspicious transactions. They found nothing, but I know how easy it is to cover financial discrepancies, at least for a little while. Why was I so honest with Dr. Blight about what I had done to Abbott? I had not admitted my role in his departure to anyone, not even Maggie. Abbott agreed to step down if it made everyone else comfortable. He was always such a boy scout, all his self-sacrificing had to be fake. He even pretended he did not know I was the cause of it all. Once Miles was removed, it was easy enough for me to get the votes to take my rightful place. Dr. Blight claps suddenly, and I jump. He is smiling and staring at something behind me. I turn to see two wait staff approaching with a large cart covered in six different silver containers of varying shape and size. The main course had finally arrived.

MAIN COURSE of ACHIEVEMENTS

4

The first item set on the table is a large pot with a silver lid. The waiter removes the top to reveal a type of risotto that looks delicious but the sight is not fooling me anymore. Beside the risotto rests a silver pan with some kind of marinated baked chicken. There is a large tray of buttered rolls, perfectly browned on the top. There is also a tray of baked salmon resting beside a large bowl of stuffed pasta, and a salad. After completely covering the table in food, the waiters disappear and Blight begins to ladle portions of each dish onto a single plate with a smile and a glow in his eyes. He looks almost maniacal as he sets the plate in front of me then prepares his own, with greater portions of course. This time he is actually drooling. The delicious smell is tempting, but I have learned my lesson, these dishes have absolutely nothing for me, and I make a note to myself to never return to this restaurant. Dr. Blight is unfazed and enjoying every bite.

"Absolutely delectable; I'm sorry you're not enjoying the meal Graves. It's quite good, at least give something else a try. Or perhaps you're more of a dessert man?" Blight suggests.

"Actually I'm not one for sweets either. I think I'd be more inclined to eat if the chef was a little more generous with the flavor." I reply. Not a single dish tasted as it should, in fact, not a single dish had taste at all but Blight could not understand my complaint. Instead, he merely shrugs and refills my wineglass.

"Well, at least you like the wine. Now that we are really getting into it, let us continue. So, once you managed to oust Abbott from his position and gain your coveted role as lead pastor, what happened next?" Blight asks and I shrug.

"Honestly, nothing happened right away, I mean it took some time for the congregation to adjust to me. Around the time of the name change to Eternal Affluence, some people claimed they felt unsure about things, and genuinely I think they just didn't want to let go of Abbott or the memory of my father. Some people just can't handle change and progress." I mutter under my breath.

"What sort of change and progress? Other than the name, I mean?" Blight asks.

"Well, I made a few adjustments to the tier of control. I kept the elder committee but I replaced most of the older members with some younger, open-minded people that viewed things from a more modern perspective. The members I replaced were long past their prime and in need of rest and retirement. It was the best thing for everyone." I explain and Blight nods.

"Ah! I see, so you found it necessary to place your friends and 'yes men' in prominent roles so as to increase compliance with your decisions?" Blight suggests and I scowl.

"No, that's not what I was doing at all; at least that wasn't my intention. I'm all for people having their own opinions, but as far as employees go, I want people who can back me on decisions." I explain.

"You mean people who won't question your logic?" Blight insists.

"I mean people who won't question godly wisdom." I counter and Blight raises an eyebrow in amusement.

"I like that. You are quite talented, Mr. Graves." Blight replies.

"Thank you … I think." I reply hesitantly, unsure of whether he is actually complementing me or not.

"Well, after you got settled in, what other changes did you make?" Blight asks to move the conversation along. Now I could explain how I increased membership and got the church flourishing to the point that we had to move to a larger building just to accommodate services.

"Well, it all really began with my initiative of inclusion. Opening the doors to everyone and teaching them that we are all God's children, and to seek the blessings that are offered to all of us." I explain proudly.

"Is that how you see things? That all people are children of God?" Blight asks.

"Absolutely, don't you?" I ask but Blight shakes his head.

"That's of no matter. I have to ask though, is there a difference in your opinion between being made by God in *His* image and being *His* child?"

Blight asks with a straight face and I force a laugh to hide my discomfort in the question.

"I'm not sure if I understand what you mean." I reply as Blight is filling his plate with a second helping from the serving trays on the table.

"Well let me put it this way, in your opinion; is there a difference between being created by God and being created by God while walking in what *He* created you for? I mean according to the *Manual*, *He* is the Creator of all, but not all are of *Him.* How do you differentiate the two?" Blight asks and I shrug and pluck a roll from my plate. I bite into it and of course, I cannot taste anything, not even the butter.

"Well, being created by God and being of God are really the same thing." I reply cautiously while wondering what Blight is getting at.

"Are they? How strange, chapters like 1JN4 of the *Manual* say differently from my understanding. By your logic, an atheist or one who doesn't believe in the Creator God as the one true God is still a part of God and the body of Christ. How would that work to be a part of something that you don't acknowledge or believe in? How can you be *of* it if you don't *follow* it?" Blight asks and I wince as my head is beginning to hurt, and I think that perhaps it is the wine.

"You're going over my head here, Doc." I reply as it suddenly occurs to me that I have no idea how long I have been here. I pull up my sleeve to read my watch and see that it is only 3:00 … but wait, is it AM or PM? That could not be right either way as I was with Maggie well after 2:00 in the afternoon. I tap the face and realize the second hand is no longer moving. I sigh and push the band back up under my cuff. For $70,000, this watch should have been ticking to hell and back. Blight seems to mistake my frustrations over my watch for something involving his question so he attempts to explain a little further.

"Perhaps I am being too philosophical and I should phrase it this way, do you see a difference between those who follow the Creator God and those who don't?" Blight asks simply.

"Well, if they weren't following God, I wouldn't see them because they wouldn't be in church." I reply and Blight wags his finger in the air again.

"No, no, no. I'm afraid that's not at all true. To follow God is not merely walking into a room, singing a few songs, and having a few scriptures read to you; anyone can do that and still take no notice of their Creator whatsoever. There is more to it than that, to follow goes much deeper into things such as honor and obedience. Do you ever notice a difference between those that go deeper and those that don't?" Blight asks and by now I am fed up with the conversation and I do not bother to hide my exasperation at these ridiculous questions anymore.

"No, I don't see a difference. If a person is making an effort to show up to service once a week and financially contribute to the house of the Lord, they're following God." I snap but Blight remains calm and composed.

"So the idea of one taking up their cross daily is, in your interpretation, to make a twenty-minute drive every Sunday morning to toss the change from their morning coffee purchase into the offering basket?" Blight asks sarcastically and for some reason this offends me though I do not know why.

Before I say anything further, I finish off my glass to get a little more boldness.

"You know, people like you that are at the top of the ladder, you look down on everyone else and think the jobs of the middle men are so easy." I begin and Blight looks at me in surprise, now I am glad to be getting a reaction out of him. "My job is not easy. I try my best to bring inspiration to people. To let them know that their sins are forgiven and to accept one another. If I talk about things like sin and condemnation all day, no one would ever listen to me! No one would ever go to church if the message is always about obedience and sacrifice! So I teach people about hope and faith which is in the Bible too so I don't see the problem." I reply in defense of my methods. Blight was not the first to criticize me for my way of ministering but no one could argue that I got results.

"I don't deny that hope and faith are important teachings, but not so important as to ignore sin and consequence all together." Blight counters and I do not know what to say. Blight sets his utensils gently on the plate and stares at me. "You teach that *all* are under the one true God and *all* will be blessed, while the *Manual* says that there is a select sort who belong to *Him* and do what *He* calls them to do. They will receive the abundance of what their hearts desire as their hearts follow God, to paraphrase. Therefore, *He* does not bless everyone in all that they do; but by your teachings, the unrighteous are blessed along with the righteous, which completely negates the purpose of confession, repentance, or even obedience. If God blesses all, why would *He* waste time addressing what one should or shouldn't do in life?" Blight asks and I toss the roll onto my full plate and stare challengingly back at him.

"You don't understand what I teach. I encourage people and let them know the importance of God's grace." I reply in weak defense to Blight's accusations.

"Application of grace can be misconstrued with abuse of it." Blight replies.

"What is that supposed to mean?" I snap back.

"I have a better idea, let us get back to our previous topic of how you were running the church and you can tell me about your oldest son and your teachings to justify his actions." Blight suggests and I try not to react.

"There is nothing to tell! My son doesn't need justification of his actions. Jay is a good young man, a college graduate with a wife and a baby on the way. He has nothing but positive prospects ahead of him." I reply in Jay's defense and Blight does not argue this as he begins to scrape the remains of each dish onto his plate, leaving the silver containers completely empty. As Blight is devouring his third helping, the busser appears to clear the table. Before Blight can claim my plate for himself, I toss the food into the plastic tub the busser is carrying and in that moment, a heavy tension falls over our table. The busser remains frozen in place staring at my plate of food among the discards. He then looks at Blight who is staring hard at me.

"It's not polite to waste food, Mr. Graves." Blight says with a slight growl.

"Well what else am I supposed to do with it? Maybe if this food was edible I wouldn't be so wasteful." I reply trying to sound bold but I can hear the quiver in my own voice. I have just crossed a line somehow. Blight forces a smile that only worsens my anxiety over the shift in the atmosphere of the dining room.

"While I can't sympathize with your complaint, I would still assume the poverty of your youth would've taught you better. Perhaps those seasons of lack in your childhood did not show you what true hunger is." Blight replies in a calm but no less threatening tone, catching me off guard. Did he actually just bring up my childhood and my family's financial struggles when I was young? The times when the bills went to collections and what little money there was went to food, yet sometimes we still did not have enough to eat. Feeling an overwhelming sense of danger, I reach for the plate in the tub, but Blight raises his hand to stop me.

"Leave it, it belongs to him now." Blight replies contemptuously as he motions to the busser who hurries back into the kitchen with the remains of my meal. I can still sense the hostility in Blight's voice and I figure it is time to calm things down.

"I didn't mean any offense. This food just doesn't do it for me." I reply and Blight smiles genuinely this time before returning his attention to his meal.

"It's alright, all is forgotten and water under the bridge as they say, with one condition though; tell me the truth about your son." Blight commands and I look away to examine the room again. I see more tables in use and it is turning out to be a busy night.

"What do you want to know?" I ask hesitantly.

"I want to know of young Jay's transgressions and what you did to cover them up." Blight replies.

"I gave Jay a choice, if he married Samantha, I would give him a nice position in the church, something easy and he could make enough money for all three of them to be comfortable. If he refused I would cut him off financially and since he'd been kicked out of school, he knew he didn't have much else to fall back on." I answer straight to the point, not wanting to dwell on the issue any further.

"Why did you have to threaten him to marry her? Didn't he love her?" Blight asks with an innocent expression and I scowl at him.

"You already know so much, so you know perfectly well that he didn't love her, I doubt he even liked her beyond what he could get from her physically. Although, in Jay's defense, if Samantha had just agreed to let me pay for the clinic trip, I wouldn't have had to take extreme measures. Of course, my son has no self-control either; he was with nearly every girl within his age range in my congregation. How would that have looked if it got out that my son was getting these girls to …" It makes me so angry I cannot even finish my sentence.

"Getting these girls to what? Forgo morality?" Blight offers. "To sell their purity, sense of worth, and morals for a physical act often misunderstood for love? I've always found sexual immorality an interesting subject, as it is so easy to corrupt the church with it. How many men and women intentionally defile their beds every night and have not a single drop of guilt when they are praising on Sunday? Then there's disease and each new generation's so-called medical breakthroughs to overcome the sicknesses developed from various sins and immoral acts but, in the end, drugs are no cure, merely a means to keep the individual alive long enough to continue sinning. I used to wonder why so many churches found it difficult to address sexual immorality among their own members; then one day I came to my own conclusions on the issue." Blight adds but does not elaborate further.

"There's no reason for churches to address things like sex in that regard, but please enlighten me on your views." I reply sarcastically. Blight smiles as he licks his fingers, savoring the last drop of the food long gone.

"To discuss immorality and sexual sins among the church brings on unwanted feelings of shame and conviction for the guilty, while the innocent believe the discussion alone is sinful enough. As a whole, the church must then come to terms with the fact that they are so far from God, that something like sex with anyone other than an individual's own spouse or acts outside of God's design of it have become the norm among them. There is nothing sinful about sex in the form of God's design or biblical teachings of it when done in a particular manner. Even the *Manual* addresses sex, especially in the chapters of SOS. Of course, that is more along the lines of intimacy between a man and woman in marriage and how one should treat their partner's body with passion and gentleness as they would their own. Immorality on the other hand is about impatience and the overwhelming temptation of the flesh; this often includes pain in and out of the sadomasochistic variety. Feeding the heat of the moment and attempting to outrun the consequences. It humors me at times how many people I've met who have lodged themselves in bondage under something like sexual immorality while ignoring all the redemptive outlets their God is offering them and still they cannot understand why they are so miserable. That's how the social narrative was altered over time, by corrupting the comprehension of biblical principles and flooding truth with the lie of acceptance to all sorts of perversity. Modern society now views the virgin as pathetic and an embarrassment. Waiting for marriage before sex is a joke because sex has become the basis of the average relationship. If the sex isn't good the relationship won't be either, according to the world. When the reality is that sex as a foundation to a relationship is about as smart as building a house on sand. At the same time, the one who has *been around the block* is supposedly living their best life, with many different sexual partners while never gaining the long-term affections or commitment they desperately yearn for in secret. Because only a fool will admit they really just want to be with someone they can trust and you can't trust someone who will share their body with anyone without long term attachment." Blight explains coolly.

"It's different now in the world. Sex outside of marriage is common, it's more than accepted, it's encouraged." I reply.

"Common does not always mean right. And accepted and encouraged by whom?" Blight asks.

"Common doesn't mean it's wrong either." I counter. "And it's accepted by society, the world, anyone who has a say in it. You can't turn on basic television now without seeing some sort of stimulant of the flesh. Even kid's shows have a little bit of sexuality in them." I explain.

"Yes it's best to get them young." Blight mumbles absently before returning to the prior subject. "Why were you so insistent that your son marry the girl he impregnated, if the new truth is that sex in any form is perfectly okay?" Blight asks.

"I knew it would go over better with the congregation. While sex outside of marriage is accepted now, a few influential religious members didn't exactly agree at the time." I reply.

"Of course, make it all nice and moral before the baby is born?" Blight suggests with a smile.

"Something like that." I reply with irritation.

"A man like you couldn't be so self-deluded though. A quick marriage does not absolve one of sin. It is more of a cosmetic solution that solves nothing underneath. What matters is the fact that your son did not love that girl, and a forced marriage did not change that. You did what you did to Jay and Samantha to save your own reputation, not to create a healthy relationship or family for your grandchild. Adding to the fact that no one sought forgiveness or repented at the time only makes matters worse." Blight explains.

"God understands our weaknesses, and His grace is enough for forgiveness." I reply, slightly offended by Blight's criticism of my actions.

"Funny thing about forgiveness, one has to first admit there is something that needs to be forgiven; and I don't believe grace works in the way you say.

Another thing I cannot understand about humanity is the adulterous nature. Does it just come naturally to bond with someone and even claim your devotion and love to them just to get what you want physically or worldly while looking for something else at the same time? Consider the Savior of the world, who gave *His* life in such a way and for reasons that are impossible for any other human being to replicate, to create a covenant, a bond in blood between God and man. To be the Mediator between Creator and creation and yet, on a smaller scale, losing one's virginity is of the same covenant in blood, meant to be between two people who become one until death. Amazing how quickly one will soil or fracture either of these bonds by giving away their devotion or their flesh to another." Blight says and I finally snap.

"It wasn't my fault!" I shout. "Linda is the one who spoiled that boy rotten!" I add and Blight presses his fingertips together calmly in contemplation.

"Oh, yes, I nearly forgot about your wife, Mrs. Graves. I found her case to be very interesting as well. Your son is her favorite child, isn't he?" Blight asks, unmoved by my outburst and accusation.

"Of course he is. She's always covering for him, defending him whenever I try to lay down some kind of authority. I did what I could to establish limits and boundaries. Even when he was a teenager, I told her if he was going to drink, make sure he did it at home. A week later my car is totaled, and I'm bailing him out of jail while struggling to keep his DUI out of the news." I complain.

"I assume your wife was covering for Jay when she suggested that the first girl he impregnated have an abortion?" Blight asks, and I answer without thinking.

"Of course she did, and who do you think got left to cover the medical bills that time? Not to mention …" I stop cold as Blight is smiling at me. How did he know about Jay's ex-girlfriend Lydia?

"Please, go on. You know what I'm going to say, so don't bother asking how I know." Blight explains. He cups his hands under his face, giving my story his full attention. I look around the room to make sure no one else is listening. A diner sitting across from us looks asleep while her companion is devouring the rest of the meal like an animal. I return my attention to Blight.

"You don't go easy on a guy do you?" I ask Blight.

"Trust me when I say that there is no better place or time than here and now to let it all out." Blight replies.

"They were both in high school at the time and she didn't want to ruin her life or his. She didn't want her parents to know about it either and she didn't have any money to handle it discreetly. I paid for her to get it done, and I covered her first year of tuition for college just to show that there were no hard feelings. It didn't do too much good for her since she dropped out of school a year later anyway." I explain and Blight laughs.

"That was merely the beginning of her troubles. Were you aware she tried to kill herself a few years later?" Blight asks. I look up sharply and shake my head. Blight's expression is full of glee as he speaks and I take another drink of wine. I should slow down, but it is good wine.

"Well, that was her decision, that's nothing on me. I did what I could for her and my son. And for the record, I find it a little strange that you're looking down on me for my stance on women's reproductive rights." I reply and Blight looks at me quizzically. More and more it seems we are on very different topics in this conversation so I try to explain further. "I know it's a touchy subject for some people, but I think it's best that the option is open to all. If you don't want to do it, don't do it, if you do want to do it, that's her choice, and it's a woman's right to choose." I add proudly.

"The right to choose what?" Blight asks.

"The right to choose … Well, you know what I'm talking about, the right to choose what she wants to do." I reply, stuttering slightly, I do not know how to respond right away as the people in my circle, including other pastors I knew, never openly questioned pro-choice or elaborated on whether it was right or wrong.

"The right to choose, life or death you mean? It's funny that so few people like to finish that sentence. As if they should be embarrassed or ashamed over the decision of who should live for whom or who should die for whom. Of course abortion is not always as simple as one life for another now is it." Blight says.

"It's not alive in the first place, so how is it dying? A person's body is their own and the Word of God is about freedom. When we take away a woman's right to choose, we take away her God-given freedom." I declare in a harsh tone. I had counseled many women and a few men on the issue when they were at a crossroads and admitted that a child would bring unwanted changes to their lives. Blight's questions on the issue make me think of Maggie, which is not a place I want to go right now. People just need to know they have options and be encouraged that whatever choice they make will be the right choice for them.

"God's Word is about life and freedom *from* sin. Imagine the effort *He* puts into each life, including designing an unborn baby for a purpose, just to have someone kill it in the womb while attempting to use *His* Word to justify the infanticide. Moreover, if it is a matter of choice, does one not have the freedom to choose some sort of preventive measures while fornicating, such as a contraceptive or prophylactic? They come in many styles and colors to choose from as well." Blight quips. "Or even the choice to abstain from sex altogether? Why must a choice be made after a life is conceived? Does the choice of life or death upon a helpless baby make one feel powerful? Or is it some sort of rebellion against God the Creator by destroying what *He* created?" Blight suggests thoughtfully. "No, that can't be it either, because I've seen too many broken after making such a choice. I wonder why you've never taught on the aftermath of an abortion and what it does to a person psychologically, emotionally, spiritually, and especially physically." Blight adds.

"I'm sure the doctors know what they are doing." I say offhandedly.

"And yet young Lydia just didn't feel the same." Blight says and I look him straight in the eye.

"That's not my business, but I pray she made her peace with the Lord." I reply smartly and Blight smirks but I ignore it.

"I do enjoy your directness; it reminds me of the eugenicists I oversaw in my past studies. Of course, their intentions were the same then as they are now only with new methods to eradicate whom they deem the undesirables of society under the guise of freedom and taking back control of one's body. I suppose the unborn don't deserve such freedom or control over their own existence? Well, let us move on. Tell me about your daughter Sasha, I believe you mentioned she was seeing someone. Is she still with … Megan, I believe that was her name? The one Sasha started dating when she admitted her feelings for other women to you and your wife." Blight details and I slam my hand down on the table hard causing my wine glass to tip over onto the floor and shatter. Blight is unfazed by my outburst and someone appears almost immediately to clean up the mess. Just as quickly, I have a new, refilled glass of wine in front of me.

"Please, Mr. Graves, let us not have any of that. There is no need for you to become hostile. As I recall you were very welcoming to Sasha's admittance of homosexuality. In fact, you spoke in one of your sermons of how proud you were of Sasha for being bold enough to admit such a thing to you and Linda. I enjoyed that one as much as your previous sermon in which you attempted to justify your son's immoral behavior. I remember them both so well I dubbed them *the teachings of transgression acceptance*." Blight says and I stare at him with pure hatred refusing to speak. Blight merely shrugs and continues. "If I remember correctly you said sex outside of marriage was perfectly acceptable now and you spoke vaguely of King David and his tryst with Bathsheba. That was the first I could recall of you applying the *Manual* in any of your teachings, although you edited the true story greatly for your purposes. You turned it into a fable of how immorality works out for good in the end by neglecting to speak of the baby Bathsheba gave birth to or her first husband's death to make way for her marriage to King David. While the true events are about sinful actions and their consequences, you used it to reinforce perversity and sin by holding back portions of the narrative." Blight adds. I turn to slide out of the booth and leave but stop when I realize my foot has gone to sleep from sitting for so long. I remain on the edge of the seat stomping my foot a few times to wake it back up.

"Please my friend, I mean no insult toward you. I only want you to recount the lessons you gave to your congregation as I found them all to be very fascinating. Let us enjoy this evening and the rest of our meal, as we still have dessert to look forward to." Blight explains with a sincere expression. Maybe he was not actually mocking me but praising my work, in his own peculiar way. I concede and pull myself back into the booth. Blight smiles and continues. "Now where were we? That's right, your teachings to justify abysmal behavior." Blight reminds himself excitedly.

"I was helping people understand the grace of God and to know that sin could and would be forgiven." I reply defensively.

"You were helping people to abuse that grace and act as if no sin had been committed so they didn't have to bother with forgiveness or repentance. Of course, many of your members were already committing sins and took comfort in your words to justify and excuse their behavior. Those who were already married found an absolving of guilt in the follow-up sermon about how adultery is not the fault of the adulterer, as God understands a person to be weak and sometimes they just have to feed the urge. You satisfied many who were guilty among your congregation and while you never even suggested the offending party end their extra-marital liaisons, you did hint the idea of returning to their spouse as a form of penance. This way they could throw away all guilt because they 'Came home to the one they *really* loved' as you put it. Therefore, the offended party must push down their feelings of bitterness and hurt while attempting to comfort themselves with the notion that though the one they love is unfaithful, they still come home. Then again, the offended party could always leave and feel the condemnation and guilt of divorce because they are unaware the adultery has already broken their marital covenant. You, Graves, are a sneaky one. In all my years of service, I've met a few like you that managed to pass the blame from the perpetrator onto the victim, but none have done so with such style. Was this the manipulation you used on your wife when she found out about your first mistress Rachel?" Blight asks. I cannot understand how he knows all of this! I had not seen Rachel in years. I do not answer right away, but I take a moment to finish off my fresh glass of wine.

"Come on Graves, keep to the deal." Blight presses and I figure, what does it matter now?

"Of course that's why I needed the sermon, you know that. I hadn't seen Rachel since my twins were in high school and Linda was still bitter about it. One day Linda found some old bank statements and paperwork about Rachel's condo that I had renovated years ago and she got upset all over again, accusing me of lying about ending it. This was a few years before I met Maggie, so honestly I was still doing my best to make my marriage work. I tried to explain to her that she had everything while Rachel had nothing, since I broke it off between us. She just looked at me as if I was crazy and asked me if I thought I deserved a medal for taking care of my wife better than my mistress. I made big sacrifices for Linda throughout our marriage but she just would not let go of the past. So one Sunday, I gave the sermon about infidelity. I figured why not use my platform to explain things? It all seemed to work just fine and everything calmed down after that." I explain as I smile to myself and pour another glass.

"What's so funny?" Blight asks with a look of amusement on his own face.

"I guess it shouldn't be funny, but thinking about it now, I don't know why I tried so hard to keep Linda around. I don't know why I put so much effort into saving our marriage when I didn't even want to marry her in the first place. I suppose being such a good preacher is a gift and a curse." I reply and now it is Blight's turn to smile.

"Your … preaching talents are not why she stayed." He replies.

"How would you know?" I snap. "You know what, never mind, I forgot you know everything." I add indignantly.

"Well in the case of your wife Linda, I trained with her caseworker. Linda's strictly religious childhood environment, religious, mind you, not relational, was perfect for an event of sexual abuse without the offsetting effects of healing. My colleague used the incident of abuse on your wife to instill in her the idea that God did not love her, but merely tolerated her and every other woman in the world. This was further progressed by her upbringing's principles against women teachers, as we manipulated the interpretation of certain chapters of the *Manual* to confuse select groups and develop an oppressive regime. The intent was to prevent at least half the human population from spreading the gospel. These teachings are what kept Linda from attending female lead groups in her later years where she might have learned of her true worth in her Creator. This also helped in her caseworker's campaign of teaching Linda that the abuse was her own fault, an idea furthered by her mother's approach to the situation in which she scolded a then 10 year-old Linda for being too attractive and seducing the man who … well, you get the idea. This also worked well generationally as Linda later criticized your daughter Ramona when she was 12 years old for her choice of pajamas at a slumber party after an adult made a pass at her and touched her inappropriately." Blight explains as he examines the other diners. I set my drink down slowly as I take in what Blight has just said.

"Linda was never abused as a child and neither was Ramona." I reply sharply. Where did he get an idea like that anyway?

"They were in fact, but that's in the past, my point is that Linda remained with you even after your indiscretions broke your marital covenant, because she feared God would hate her even more if she left, as she had developed a mindset during your marriage that she was nothing without you. She also convinced herself to blame your mistresses for your straying, as she was taught that all women are natural-born seducers, much like Delilah was to

Samson or as Jezebel was to the church in chapter RE2 of the *Manual*, and that men could not be held accountable for their lustful actions." Blight explains smoothly, I almost believe what he is saying as the waiter appears with a fresh bottle, and I refill my glass.

"None of that stuff happened to my wife, if it had she would've told me. She stayed because she knew what I said was the truth." I reply.

"Would you have listened if she told you? A better question is would you have believed her?" Blight asks and I look at Blight's hands on the table and frown. He is not even married, but he is trying to tell me about how to be a good husband. At least I know my role. "Whether you believe me or not, I only bring up the incident to explain your wife's history. You're not to blame for what happened regarding the abuse itself, but you did play off of it for your own benefit." Blight adds, his tone not accusatory but more matter-of-fact as if there is no point in my arguing about it.

"How could I have played off of anything I didn't know about?" I ask and Blight smiles.

"How indeed? Either way, Linda's mother and assaulter were the main parties used in Linda's conditioning. In fact, I'm a great fan of your mother-in-law, she was in what I call the elderly influencer circle. Mainly for the way her neglectful attitude as a mother affected Linda, who then passed down her own silent aggressions and bitterness to her own daughters. Linda, her mother and so many other women like them fail to see that their assignment on earth includes being great spiritual warriors, like modern-day Deborahs; yet they waste all their Spirit-given gifts, strength, wisdom and authority on belittling each other and fighting the male influencers for the inheritance, they think God is denying them. Some women are so quick to forget all the trials of their own youth when they were navigating through a harsh world that promoted sex and unattainable beauty standards on them as life-defining traits. They have absolutely no sympathy for the next generation of their gender. Making matters worse, as the next generation seeks companionship among spoiled brutes that would say anything just to get to the flesh beneath their pretty, little clothes and disappear as fast by morning, leaving the poor girls more detached and forlorn than when they started. Through this form of low self-esteem and self-hate my colleague managed to create in your wife a sort of maternal imbalance as she is affectionate, understanding, and compassionate to Jay and his indiscretions but has absolutely no patience for your daughter's. As I recall, Linda was completely against your teachings about acceptance of homosexuality but seemed to have no complaints about Jay and his fornications." Blight reminds me and I take a moment to consider his words. He was right, Linda was against my teaching about the acceptance of homosexuality, as she hated when I approved of anything Sasha did.

"I hope the wine is not getting to you just yet. It's your favorite and you tend to overindulge often." Blight cautions.

"I told you I don't like white wine." I reply with a straight face.

"I meant the contents. Its ingredients are of your preference, so to speak. But now you must have another glass, as the desserts have arrived." Blight exclaims as another large tray arrives at our table.

JUST DESSERTS

5

Two large platters are set on the table, the first platter holds a full strawberry cheesecake and the other is a full chocolate cake. I turn away, annoyed by the delicious appearance of the desserts, knowing they are very likely not as they seem. Blight cuts a slice of both cakes, setting them on a single plate before me. Against my better judgment, I delicately press my fork into the dessert, collecting a small amount of the tender chocolate crumbs on the prongs. I close my lips over the chocolate and press my tongue down on the moist cake. Not a single tang of cocoa, sweet sugar, rich butter or whatever else should have made up a delicious cake. In anger, I spit the cake bits out into my napkin and toss it on the table.

"Oh dear, can't stand the dessert either, I see. The chef will be so disappointed." Blight replies as he takes his time with this portion, perhaps because he is finally getting full. Considering how much he ate already, it is a wonder he can still breathe.

"You said something before about my wife having a case worker. She never had any case worker for anything." I reply to change the subject and Blight holds his fork in the air as if considering.

"She had no case worker that you would know of until now, but she did have one, does still have one actually, but their job has gotten a bit difficult lately as they don't have you around anymore to fan the flames in a way. Of course, I'm hoping to have all that rectified by the end of this dinner. As for now, my colleagues and I are still trying to salvage the seeds planted through you or at least nurture them a little while longer. I'm happy to say that Jay and Sasha are still active under our influence for the time being and young Braden has a great deal of potential, but things are still looking grim. I do wonder though, what went through your mind when you told your congregation about your oldest daughter's sexual orientation?" Blight asks. I shrug before taking another drink of wine while pushing my plate across the table to Blight's welcoming hands.

"I just explained to everyone that love is love, no matter what. What's important is that it's mutual. I told my congregation that just because God had at one time condemned homosexuality, that didn't mean He still did so now. It's important to me to catch the church up with the rest of the world." I explain.

"And this didn't bother your congregation at the time, the fact that you were ignoring many chapters of the *Manual* including verses from RO1?" Blight asks.

"Of course it offended a few people and they left the church, but we were better off without them. I won't have hatemongers trying to force severe conservative views in my congregation." I reply harshly.

"You offended more than a few people, actually a significant number of your original congregation's members left but I'm surprised you noticed at all since their seats were soon filled with people who found you to agree with their current lifestyles. The new members got real comfortable with your teachings and became walking contradictions." Blight jokes.

"And I have no regrets about that. It's all love, maybe just a different kind of love, but that doesn't make it a sin." I reply defiantly.

"Yes, well *difference* is not what makes sin, sin in the first place." Blight counters.

"Then what does?" I snap. Blight is again unfazed by my sharp tone.

"I believe you mean, *who* does, and as a teacher of *His* Word, I would think you would know that *He* does not change *His* mind on sin. Of course, you are completely uneducated in the *Manual* itself and you have only gotten as far as you have in the role of influencer because the people that follow you are even *less* educated in the Word of God." Blight replies.

"Hey, you don't have the right to judge me for any of the decisions I've made or my teachings, and what is this Manual you keep talking about?" I ask and Blight takes another bite of his cake, chewing slowly as he stares at me.

"Exactly my point, but once again I must stress the fact that I am not judging you for your actions or anything else really, as that is not my job. I am merely going over the facts and to be honest I can relate with you on these subjects, including that of your daughters. Sasha blindsided you with her lifestyle announcement so what else could you do but preach acceptance of it." Blight suggests in an understanding tone and I pour myself another drink.

"What else could I do? She comes to me one day out of the blue, crying about how I treat Jay so much better than her. How we let him bring Samantha over to the house but Sasha can't bring her girlfriend. Sometimes I just don't have the energy for that girl, I mean, she's so starved for attention. A part of me just knew the whole thing was for show, her being a lesbian and all, she was only doing it to make drama, but I knew there was no point in calling her out on it. I figured, forget it, take a chance, preach about inclusion, and it worked out. Our numbers doubled and then tripled. The money grew too, but I was already paying out so much more for everything else I hardly noticed the increase. You wouldn't believe what I sacrifice for my kids just to have them be so unappreciative." I add in a moment of self-pity and Blight smiles.

"I doubt you're the only father with such unappreciative children." Dr. Blight replies and I act as if I did not hear him. What did I care about other fathers?

"And even after all that, the ungrateful little brat has the nerve to accuse me of only preaching acceptance because I didn't want to get cancelled." I add bitterly.

"Well, she wasn't wrong. Like anyone else in the spotlight, you did do it for the numbers and the acceptance." Blight replies flatly.

"Well of course I did, but she didn't have to accuse me of it!" I shout but the other diners do not react to my outburst. In fact, the dining room is now full, but I realize for the first time what is missing from the moment I walked in: no chattering, no sound, no other conversations but our own. Nearly every table occupied, and I can see people talking, I can see their lips moving, but I cannot hear a single sound from any of them. I try to lean over to the table nearest us, but Blight interjects.

"Their conversation is none of your concern, just as ours, is none of theirs. I told you this was a private affair so you should have no fears over what you share with me." Blight assures me again and I sit back in the booth and close my eyes.

"Of course I did it for the numbers, what other reason would I have for teaching something so ridiculous? I mean I don't have a problem with gay people, I just wouldn't take part in a lifestyle like that myself and honestly it still seems unnatural to me, just looking at that sort of thing makes me cringe. Still, I have to accept that it's a new world and I figure plenty of people are looking for a church that respects their way of living. I took a bet back then and it paid off, and nobody needs to know my personal feelings on the subject." I explain.

"I agree some people are looking for a church that respects their lifestyle, or more so, compromises the Word of God to *justify* their lifestyle." Dr. Blight comments and I shrug, feeling a little tired and not caring at this point if he is judging me or not. "Still, I understand it is a complicated issue. Many believe they can remain in any way of life and still love God. They forget that real love requires sacrifice and understanding at times. Real love requires honesty and work too. Some people choose a type of *loving* God the way they want to and not the way they truly should. You know while I'm not sure how it began for others, Sasha's case worker was very detailed in instilling in her bitterness and feelings of neglect through you and Linda. Eventually leading Sasha to disregard the God she grew to believe hated her as much as you did. In reciprocation to this disdain, she believed both *He* and you carried for her, Sasha would do what she could to defy you, Linda and her Creator as revenge for making her something unlovable. As your son's choices led you to teach your congregation that sexual immorality or sex outside of marriage was the new norm and acceptable in God's eyes, Sasha's lifestyle led you to declare the same about homosexuality. Additionally her caseworker used various encounters with crude, perverse men to create a universal image mirroring that of the twin brother she despised. Sasha would visualize *all* men as rejecting, brutish, perverse, only-after-the-flesh beasts and users who wouldn't love her or care for her in any decent manner. To her, masculinity was equivalent to criminality, and femininity was a curse or a weakness. Over the years, Sasha was guided to associate the opposite gender with victimizers and oppressors, so that she reflected these characteristics on every male pronoun she was aware of, including her Savior. Best to let her push *Him* away, believing that *He* had rejected her first, so she would seek acceptance in relations with other women. This plan is one of many that has been proven quite effective in corrupting churches and individuals across the globe with the acceptance of homosexuality. If one can get an entire congregation to ignore very clear and precise commands in the *Manual* just so they can fill up the collection baskets and avoid protests, one can get rootless influencers to do anything in unrighteousness. What matters is that people like you focus on the monetary profit in acceptance of sinful things while ignoring the mental, spiritual, physical, emotional, and generational damage sexual immorality and other such sins cost all of humanity. So many of you foolishly believe there is much to profit in gaining the whole world while losing your own soul as addressed in MK8 of the *Manual*." Blight explains while finishing off another slice of cake. Unable to resist, I begin to laugh uncontrollably. Blight merely smiles in return.

"You are the strangest doctor I have ever met. Were you some kind of psychology major that had a soft spot for theology in school?" I ask, trying to understand the unusual combination of topics.

"You could say that. I've had a great deal of university training and even more time in on-site experience." Blight replies as he cuts another slice of both cakes.

"So now what? Honestly, I can't seem to tell whether or not you want to work with me." I confess. Even if I do not get this job there are other places out there for me, so I will just keep looking if I have to. A strange interview is not enough to interrupt my comeback, and at least now, I will have a wild story to tell.

"Why would you guess that I don't want to work with you? I've been working with you all this time." Blight replies, visibly confused.

"How so?" I ask equally confused.

"Well this evening alone you've given me at least some insight into what to do next. You see even though we have a firm grip on your twins and youngest son, young Ramona is the persistent hold out. Even after all of your teachings, Ramona refuses to accept the compromised gospel. She sought the truth, eventually sharing real lessons and salvation with your mother before her death and so another one was lost to us and I fear more of your family members will follow, which is quite problematic for me. What it all comes down to is that when *He* is involved it's very hindering to my work." Blight replies bitterly and it is the first time all night that I have seen him look intimidated by something or someone.

"*He*? Who is *He*?" I ask Dr. Blight who is staring across the room at the other diners. The doctor continues speaking as if he did not hear me at all.

"I must admit that you gave me great advantage in my work for years, Mr. Graves. You were a door to many possibilities and kept us well fed down here, but as I feared, even the best of vessels soon lose their use. I suppose it has much to do with MW7 and such chapters like it of the *Manual*, to examine someone by their fruits. Bad deeds cannot produce good outcomes, and many former members of your congregation came to realize this when they compared your teachings to the *Manual* itself. Young Ramona took me completely by surprise though, as did your mother and her reception of what Ramona shared with her. I underestimated Ramona greatly, and at this point, my superiors are near to deeming my work within your family to be a complete failure. You see, while your mother had her own disillusions to the gospel, as she and your father began the church with good intentions but were eventually led astray by greed and other factors, it was after her stroke that she learned humility and guilt for her past. She also learned the truth about the love and grace of God through Ramona's care for her. She accepted Christ as her Savior and learned to pray with Ramona, seeking God's forgiveness for her own sins. She would pray for you, your wife and your children, asking God to forgive her for where she failed as an example to you. She wanted you to be a better man than your father, to be an honest man of God." Blight confesses and I scowl as I take a drink. What an arrogant old woman to think I needed her prayers for anything!

"What is it with you, and my mother, and my daughter Ramona? Why do you keep bringing them up?" I ask and Dr. Blight looks at me with a faint hint of surprise.

"I only mean to explain the difficulties I've been having with your family lately. I'm sure you were aware of what happened to Ramona after she left your church?" Blight asks and I pour another glass to stop myself from throwing the bottle at him.

"I don't need to be aware of anything Ramona did after she abandoned her family." I reply bitterly and Blight smiles.

"Come on now, Graves. You and I both know that's not what she did at all, she was simply doing what she knew to be right. As the *Manual* says in 1JN4, one must test the spirits, and she did just that after your teachings of inclusion. She found that things were not as you tried to sell them. In fact, right before your fall from grace, didn't she attempt to make amends with you?" Blight asks.

"Calling me a false prophet and an idolater is not what I would consider making amends." I reply sharply.

"Did she call you all that? As I remember she merely brought up how none of your teachings actually referenced the Word of God and you called her a baby in the faith and told her she had no right to minister to someone like yourself about the Scriptures." Blight recounts.

"You got that right, I did tell her all of that, and I'd tell her again if I had the chance. She was all of what, sixteen, seventeen years old, and she thought she had the right to teach me something. Young people nowadays think they know everything," I explain.

"You know I was counting on you reacting that way when she tried to talk to you. People like you are the best recipients to pride as your age or the years you've been saved seem to be the deciding factors on your own wisdom, not how much you spend learning the Word of God or what you do with it. I once had a case where a man was living in immorality with his long-time girlfriend and thought nothing of it. He was baptized when he was five, and by then being fifty years old, he didn't have to do anything else, according to his own logic and beliefs. When his son brought this ungodly lifestyle to his attention, the father was too busy trying to figure out which one of his ancestors committed a sin that God was currently punishing the father for, through disease, in his own flawed interpretation of generational sin. This, of course, was more so a cop out to the fact that the current sin was in the old man himself and not his ancestors. By focusing on someone he'd never met who was long dead, the father wouldn't have to acknowledge that the man himself had let our kind in with his own unrighteous and immoral living. I should add that the son had been saved only a few months prior to the confrontation between them, and the old man was quick to tell the boy that he had no idea what he was talking about and not to preach to a seasoned believer when the boy himself was still just a baby. Pride leads a person to think their long life makes them all knowing and wiser so they discount anything a new believer has to say. You reacted the same way to Ramona and like that old man, you also have been counted among our numbers because pride and offense blinded you from the truth that was offered to you on many occasions." Blight explains.

"What do you mean about truth being offered to me? Ramona was a child; she didn't know what she was talking about." I argue.

"If God can speak to a prophet through a donkey as *He* did in chapter NU22 of the *Manual*, I would think *He* could use a child to bring truth to you if *He* wanted to. Either way I was glad you chose to insult her instead, rejecting everything she said to you as that could have uprooted all my plans much earlier and I could have lost you along with your mother. I even attempted to use the encounter to corrupt Ramona's mind with bitterness toward you over your insults, but she was unmoved and merely cried out to *Him* asking for help to save her family." Blight replies crossly.

"I still don't see the point of you reminding me that she left and I still don't understand why you keep bringing her up? I thought this meeting was about you and me." I explain.

"You don't blame her for your undoing, do you? It was not her pulling away that ruined you." Blight replies, trying to deflect my question.

"Ramona couldn't have removed me from Eternal Affluence, even if she wanted to. I stepped down willingly, remember?" I remind Blight who nods.

"I remember it well as a matter of fact. It was after Miss Rachel came forward with all the lurid details of your past relationship and so many other things you did in the past to save your reputation. After that, it seemed as though everything started coming undone. Even Maggie was a little upset at you after learning that she was not the first of your extramarital relationships. By then the flood gates of your indiscretions seemed to burst open and reveal everything and as the *Manual* says in chapter LU12, 'There is nothing covered that will not be revealed.'" Blight quotes and I glare at him for mocking my ousting. He merely smirks and finishes his cake. As soon as he sets his utensils down the busser returns to collect the empty plates. A waiter soon follows with a bowl of mints and the check.

AFTER DINNER REFLECTIONS

6

Dr. Blight removes the pen from the book and as I think he is going to sign, instead he pokes himself in the thumb and presses his bloody thumbprint onto the paper. I wince as I have always hated the sight of blood, but what is more unusual than how he pays is that Blight's blood is not red but black, black as ink in fact. Blight hands the check back to the waiter who disappears with it. Blight opens a single mint from the little ceramic bowl and pops it into his mouth. I do not bother to try them as I have come to accept that there is nothing for me in this entire restaurant aside from the wine.

"You know, you're very confusing. This whole dinner has just been up and down all night. On some points, you praise me for my work and on other points, you criticize me, and I don't get it. So maybe we can just end this like gentlemen by you being straight with me as to whether you're interested in partnering with me or not?" I ask and Blight looks at me quizzically.

"Partner with you?" Blight eventually asks after a dramatic moment of silence.

"To join your organization; this was an assessment to my qualifications for a lead position, right?" I add and Blight stares at me while licking his lips.

He smiles and his eyes light up as he begins to chuckle then his body begins to shake with full on laughter from his gut. He begins to slam his hand down on the table repeatedly causing my wine glass and the bottle to bounce across the table. I feel uneasy until I remember that the other patrons cannot hear us, they are unfazed and remain deep in their own conversations. A few more diners seem to have fallen asleep in their seats while their companions continue eating the awful food. I am completely confused on what Blight finds so funny.

"You, Mr. Graves are by far the best interview I have ever had." Blight admits after he has had a moment to catch his breath.

"Well, I'll take that as a compliment." I reply indignantly as all my plans seem to be coming undone tonight.

"And you should, for the simple fact that I have a tendency to grow bored in my work. Some of my clients are so malleable and rootless that it's almost as if I have to do nothing at all to steer them. I'm so used to people who have no will of their own, no real drive, but you Mr. Graves, I find to be a worthy cause. And now that we're finally face to face after all this time, you believe that I called you down here for some sort of merger?" Blight asks and I sit up in anger.

"You did call me here! You said you wanted an assessment of my work!" I remind him.

"True, I did call you here for an assessment, not of your work though, of mine, for my superiors so that I may continue my work within the rest of your family." Blight explains slowly and my stomach drops.

"What are you talking about? What does my family have to do with all of this? This has nothing to do with them." I snap back.

"My job has everything to do with them now, as I've invested a great deal of time in your household and your congregation, and it's important to me that I am able to see it through." Blight explains.

I sit back in my seat and sulk about the time wasted. This never would have happened if I had not stepped down from leading Eternal Affluence. If I had not let them push me out of what I built. That church was nothing until I got a hold of it and managed to make it into more than just a building full of people, but an empire.

"So I wasted all this time here just so *you* could get some sort of promotion?" I ask, not bothering to hide my hostility. Blight tosses another mint into his mouth and stares at me while remaining silent. "I bet you think you're real important, some kind of big shot calling me all the way down here to this awful restaurant with their bland and flavorless food, then you have the nerve to laugh at me like this was some kind of prank." I add and Blight looks away.

"My apologies for finding the misunderstanding humorous, but as far as the food is concerned, it has taste and flavor, very good flavor I might add, it is merely acquired, as I said before." Blight replies. I shake my head and pluck a mint from the bowl.

"Acquired? Yeah right. I still don't understand why you can't offer me something. You said I had what you needed, and then you have me come all the way down here for nothing. I even turned down a previous offer just to be here to meet you." I snap and Blight frowns.

"I'm aware. In fact you turned down many offers and encounters to be here, but that was your own choice." Blight replies as he takes a tablet out of the briefcase on the seat beside him and begins to write something down.

"So why did you waste my time? You think I have nothing better to do?" I ask and Blight looks at me.

"I know you have nothing better to do. And it was necessary for you to make it here either way." Blight replies.

"I don't see why, if there is no place for me here; I might as well go back home." I reply.

"Oh, there is indeed a place for you here, but if there wasn't, how exactly would you plan to accomplish an impossible task such as returning to your old home? A better question, do you even know where your home is now?" Blight challenges and I sit back in my seat.

"The same place I left it. 721 Green Avenue." I reply boldly and Blight smiles.

"Mr. Graves, you grow more and more intriguing by the minute. In fact, I find you so intriguing that I'm going to do something I've never done before." Blight says.

"I hope it involves setting me up with something good here and preferably within walking distance to a decent restaurant." I suggest but Blight does not seem to hear me.

"Look around the room." Blight commands and I look around at all the other tables and see that each party has one person who has fallen asleep in their chair while the other person is ravenously devouring the rest of the meal.

"Why are all these people asleep?" I ask.

"It's more a sedation due to heavy marinating, so to speak. They can all hear and feel but they cannot move. Like you, the sedated individuals came here for assessments performed by my colleagues and myself, my colleagues would be the ones you see devouring the food, as they are enjoying the fruits of their labors. Come with me." Blight directs and I slide out of the booth. I take the wine bottle with me as I follow Blight to the back of the restaurant where there is nearly no light at all. I thought the front room was bad but this is like some sort of cavern. Each table holds a single lamp with a strange red luminescence. I can make out at least three or four forms sitting in the seats per table with at least a dozen red lamps marking each table. The further back the room goes, the darker it seems to get. I stop to allow my eyes to adjust to make out more of the figures sitting at the tables, their faces heavily obscured by the darkness, but Blight gently grabs my arm and steers me toward the kitchen.

COMPLIMENTS TO THE CHEF

7

The kitchen décor matches the black and white layout and dim lighting of the main dining room. I can barely see the figures of the waiters rushing back and forth, to collect plates and drop off order tickets because it is so poorly lit. Blight stops beside a counter to watch the cooks about ten feet away from us, hidden from the waist down by the large grills and stoves surrounding them.

"You new arrivals are all the same; at least the few of you who believe this place exists. You come here all excited and thinking you have a future because you have no idea how this place works. You are just like every other diner in here tonight Mr. Graves, all big talk on earth and then you end up here and still believe you're in some kind of position of power. Believing you're still wealthy, or young, or beautiful or influential, whatever else you may have had pride in or worshiped instead of God. Thinking all those worldly possessions you gained in life would follow you to the other side. 721 Green Avenue used to be your home many years ago, but it is not anymore. Your wife and children don't even live there now." Blight reveals.

"I don't see how Linda could've moved out that fast if I saw her just this morning. In fact, we got into an argument before I left to see Maggie." I reply quickly to catch him up.

"Check your phone." Blight replies.

"I don't have it. I left it in my car." I reply smugly.

"Down here, you don't have a car, and your phone is in the left pocket of your *charcoal suit jacket*." Blight replies emphatically and I suddenly feel the weight of my phone in the left pocket of my charcoal suit jacket. I pull the device out slowly knowing perfectly well that I did not have it when I arrived here.

"Neither did you have your watch which is no longer working, just like your phone. You were also without your coveted charcoal gray suit. When I saw yours up there with the living I just had to get one of my own. You arrived to the restaurant in what you were buried in nearly ten years ago. It seems Linda wasn't all too fussy when it came to your burial or perhaps she thought it best to bury you in the very same suit you were wearing when you died in Maggie's condominium. My apologies for the delay in our meeting, as I have quite the backlog of assessments and the remaining members of your family have kept me incredibly busy." Blight replies.

"You're lying. I haven't been here ten years." I say, sure that this is all some ridiculous joke or hazing of the new person. Blight shrugs then raises his matching gold watch in the air.

"You haven't been *here* for ten years because time has no meaning here as you know it. It is only used in cases like yours to present a certain level of comfort and normalcy during an assessment. Much like the way I present myself here now and just as your suit changed upon your entering the restaurant, your watch appeared and your phone by your side as they, like time in general, are things that you couldn't be without in your human form and have always assisted in some way to your pride, vanity, distractions and greed. However, I am not lying to you when I say you have been gone from earth for nearly ten years. In that time, your wife Linda has remarried an interesting sort. He's not a believer, but she has high hopes for him, as do we. Your son Jay is going through a bitter divorce and custody battle as the young woman you forced him to marry finally got fed up with his infidelities around the same time Jay realized he actually enjoyed fatherhood and wanted to do a better job than you ever did. Sasha has bounced from one volatile relationship to another and much like her twin brother, she turns to one-night stands and alcoholism to numb the pain and feelings of constant rejection. Your youngest son, Braden, has gone on to become quite the notorious atheist as he watched your corrupted teachings with anger and has dedicated much of his adult life to disproving anything and everything related to the God he grew to doubt and disbelieve in entirely under your influence. He also got a brain tumor some years ago and swore if it came back that he would kill himself in an attempt to take back some control over his life and body. I suppose that is his right to choose, as you would say. Then there is Maggie, she *was* indeed pregnant but after your downfall and subsequent death in her home, well let's just say she saw no reason to keep the baby as she only got pregnant so you would marry her, but I'm sure you don't care about all that now. Her caseworker thanks you by the way. As I mentioned before, it is Ramona that I have had the most trouble with, which is why you and I are here. My superiors requested that I interview you in regards to my work to find some way of breaking your daughter, as I still consider you to be one of my greater successes in corruption, while I was your case worker." Blight explains as he plucks a roll off an outgoing tray and stares at me.

"This is a joke, right?" I ask honestly.

"Don't tell me you didn't know you were dead?" Blight asks.

"Of course I know! I'm not an idiot; I remember the heart attack in Maggie's bathroom!" I shout.

"I suggest you correct your tone and explain what you are so angry about then." Blight replies calmly.

"The last thing I remember is my death while I was at Maggie's place. After the watch and the pregnancy test in the trash can. I heard things and I rejected them before you called me because I knew that with my talents I was better off being a leader in hell than a servant in heaven." I reply and for the first time Blight actually looks shocked.

"You mean to tell me that you were intentionally attempting to gain some sort of rank or position here in *hell* because of the corruption you sowed on earth? And something top level at that?" Blight smiles and I flush with embarrassment again. I did not find this funny at all.

"You think this is funny? I could work circles around you any day. I'm good at what I do and I deserve to be leading something here. You said it yourself that I was talented in twisting the Scriptures for my own benefit." I reply.

"I did say you were talented; you were very talented in being used by me to twist the contents of the *Manual*. I was the puppeteer and you were the puppet. All you did, you did because I led you to do it, and you enjoyed it. What you said, you said it because I put it in your mind and on your lips to say. I played off the memories of your childhood, editing what I could so you would remember the lack and not the provision. So you would grow to chase money and profit anyway you could, including misuse of a calling that was not your own. Moreover, in the rare occasions you managed to remember when God took care of you, I made sure that you turned from gratitude and focused on your wounded pride. Instead of thanking your God for doing something for you, you would instead be angry that you couldn't do it for yourself. I molded you from the very beginning to climb the ranks until you were leading an entire congregation into the pit with us." Blight says and his brutal admission knocks the wind out of me. I came here thinking that I could make something of what was left of my reputation. Now I am learning that all my bold decisions were not at all my own but that I was led by Blight to make them.

"This isn't right; you're lying. Everything I did wasn't from you, nobody controls me. I chose to do what I did. I chose to profit the way I did and I was always in control." I reply and Blight grabs a passing busser by the arm.

"Bring a menu." Blight orders and the busser flees from the kitchen to do what he is told. I stand uncomfortably in the center of the kitchen with Dr.

Blight staring at me challengingly as we wait for the busser to return. It feels like hours but is only seconds as the busser reappears to hand the menu to Blight and hurries off again to parts unknown. Blight removes a page from the leather booklet and holds the loose page of the menu up against a low hanging sconce on the wall so the light bleeds through the page and illuminates the printing.

"Read that will you?" Blight orders and I step in close to read the names of the dishes listed.

"What is this?" I ask as I can see that the writing is not dish names as I assumed but actual signatures. Some neater than others, some larger, some smaller but every single one is someone's signed name.

"Those names, Mr. Graves, are those of your congregation who made a choice similar to your own. They chose to forgo the warnings of the *Manual* and follow your corrupted teachings instead, which they knew to be corrupted because they wanted to justify their own sinful actions and pleasures. Their choice was to follow you and in doing so they hardened their hearts to *Him* and signed themselves over to us to be devoured." Blight explains with a grim smile and I step back as I can hear a subtle growl in Dr. Blight's voice.

"So all the food …" I begin and Blight finishes my thought.

"Consisted of the best parts of your deceased followers and their sins; and they were delicious." Blight replies. This is all wrong; this is not what I imagined the place to be like before I arrived here. There must still be a way to salvage my plans.

"Again, if I led all these people to you, to feed you and your kind, then why can't I have a place here? I should be honored here!" I argue, feeling myself growing a little dizzy as I speak.

"You're absolutely right, and you will be. Just not in the way you imagined. Actually, what will happen to you here is not the way any of you imagined. The people you saw sleeping in the dining room were all sowing corruption just like you in one form or another and believed this place to be much different. They came here to celebrate their evil deeds, believing they would be welcomed among us as equals. You, on the other hand, didn't come here to be an equal, you came here to be honored. I don't deny that you would be an interesting fit here if that sort of thing could work, but there are too many negating factors, one being that you could not taste the food. It has no flavor to you, no nourishment, and in fact, beyond its appearance, you have no desire for it. Now while the sins of your followers may have profited you on earth, here they do nothing for you and you have nothing on which to survive." Blight explains.

"Arrangements can be made, for someone like me, arrangements should be made." I argue.

"Mr. Graves, let me explain something to you a little further. I am a top level corrupter in this kingdom. My job is to corrupt humans like you who have everything and still want more. We feed off you and your sinful behavior while there is still time and opportunity because that is all my kind has left. My kind are like the roaring lion of chapter 1P5 in the *Manual*, seeking whom we may devour, but it is only done so with permission.

Through the ages, we have used everything, including what you call the *Bible*, as our instructional *Manual* essentially done in reverse to corrupt every human being ever born. Still, to continue in being corrupted, one must reject salvation repeatedly in life and open themselves up to us. This is all that you managed to accomplish in your time on earth; I established everything else. I played off your vanity, your past, your flesh, and your weaknesses, as I do to every other human being on the earth that is under my charge, because it is my job and I am good at it. You were merely the next generation within the Influencer Program, where our organization builds up various members of human civilization into places of leadership, guiding, mentoring and teaching. These people of high-ranking influence can direct the rest of humanity into a downward spiral, rejecting their Creator and *His* Word. Now, of course, I'm sure you're aware that this has been going on since the beginning of time. While our kind live to encourage sinful lifestyles, it wasn't until the Influencer Program that a plan of corruption on such a massive scale was discovered. Influencing sin in a single average believer or non-believer, who might share such sins in commonality and acceptance with a few others, as Eve shared her disobedience with Adam, just didn't cut it anymore. It's a nice treat when we collect a willing soul for hell. It's a special occasion when we collect a few who thought they were going to heaven but they ignored the truth and instead end up in hell. It is a celebration though, when one not only sins purposefully, but teaches that sin to many others so that an entire family, congregation, neighborhood, region, or even nation, goes to hell because they lived believing God had changed His mind on what was good and what was bad; that is a precious moment beyond your human understanding." Blight explains cheerfully. I lean against the counter, exhausted but hoping the posture will show my contempt for him and his speech, but he continues while taking no notice of my attitude.

"Disappointingly for me, establishing the Influencer Program kept me in study much longer than I had hoped and my residency was extended into cross training in commander-level corruption. The move took me away from all pastoral and family units for a time and placed me back among the elite individuals of the world such as politicians, kings, queens, and leaders of many cultural and financial empires. A job someone like you being on the outside might find exciting but, to my dismay, I was bored there. Don't get me wrong, it had its challenges. As the *Curriculum Manual* states in PR21, God controls the hearts of leaders. *He* can steer them where *He* wishes which is quite true. You wouldn't believe how many government officials do the things they do without even understanding why or how many actually have a heart for the people they're leading. It doesn't mean they can't be lured off the path with a little power or greed to tempt them but that never really did much damage in our favor that couldn't be undone or used by God anyway. So most of my days were spent turning the *public* against its leaders, getting them to forgo the words of JU about speaking evil of those entrusted over them. It's easy enough to get a human to criticize another about their decisions when the critic has never had to make those same decisions themselves. It's even easier to get the people to complain about a leader's choices, because the people complaining have never had to make a costly decision or deal with the aftermath. This worked for a while, but once again, I soon lost interest in the trend. I needed a thrill, a challenge, and from my current position in the program it was birthed, in the age of compromise." Blight explains but I am finding it difficult to concentrate now and keep up with what he is saying.

"Wait a minute, just hold on …" I prepare to say something more but my legs give out from under me and I nearly drop the bottle of wine as I sink to the floor. Blight grips my arm tight and sets me in a seated position on the ground.

"I see this is all going over your head again. Is it a bit too much to handle? Well it seems the wine took a little longer than it should to affect you. It saddens me to say that our time together is ending, so let me continue before I lose you completely. You see, leaders are in a bind, whenever a leader makes the decision to lean to one side, the other side calls foul, dragging that leader's name through the mud and thus making them a social monster or an enemy of the country. Over time, I learned to place seeds of compromise in leaders, affecting their decisions to the point of them doing nothing at all just to avoid angering anyone. This idea was then passed down to the common citizens of the rest of the world, under the guise of woke culture and respecting all people. It began with the creation of things that should not exist, such as new expressions of perversity, and normalizing such actions so that they become common and accepted within the next generation. So that in just a few years, any individual could identify with a demographic in which they could claim oppression. For example, a man under our influence of self-rejection in our *New Man Program* decides to live as a woman because he does not understand God's love and intentions for him as the man in which God made him. The man tries to change who he is through the minimal so-called breakthroughs of human science and medicine, but deep down he knows he is still a man and cannot find a purpose for himself while posing as a woman. Therefore, he creates a purpose in activism and protesting, bullying the way into schools and eventually the malleable minds of youth under the guise of teaching acceptance and celebration to gender confusion. The corrupted man is driven by the offenses we plant in him when someone addresses him with male pronouns or calls him by his birth name. Now mind you, this causes chaos in itself as a person can come under a great deal of attack by merely referring to a man as a man, who once looked like a man and who is biologically still a man, yet that man no longer identifies as a man. Therefore, the reinvented individual makes himself a victim and takes to social destruction of anyone who refers to him by his *dead* identity. It seemed far-fetched and foolish at the time except, as you know, the plan is actually working. People have begun to accept this forced new social construct, claiming that to reject such a thing is oppressive to people who feel this way, ignoring the spiritual and psychological oppression in individuals whom we attack with this self-rejection. This also leads to gender oppression of such groups as natural born women who will lose their rights in a world trying to cater to men trying to become women or vice versa. Gender identity soon became another aspect of human nature that we were able to use to create division, further distancing the Creator from *His* creations. Then the rest of the world must comply with the social change, causing people to walk on philosophical eggshells about issues that should not exist, while ignoring the continuing imbalance of issues that do. Take for instance the roots of infanticide that go all the way back to chapter EX1 of the *Manual*, not to mention eugenics and forced sterilizations based off of race and mental capabilities, but we don't have time to go further into that. All this is only easy to apply in the way of corruption, because humans are now desperate not to offend anyone with a platform. They have yet to grasp the fact that avoiding offense is impossible. To agree with one thing is to disagree with another. To protest one thing is to promote another. One cannot please everyone, and if your opinion differs from the loudest of the masses, the witch-hunt begins. I once had a case where an influencer got offended when they realized someone was *trying* not to offend them and it offended them that they seemed easily offended. I still can't think about that case with a straight face." Blight explains thoroughly before tossing another mint from his pocket into his mouth and smiling down at me.

"What's happening to me?" I ask as I can barely move my arms and my lower body is immobile. Blight holds his hand up to silence me.

"Just hold on, we're nearly done here. Another example of my work in this new culture is that God is against gender and racial divides. *He* made the entire world in *His* image, every color, ethnicity, generation and either gender should represent *Him* and glorify *Him*. Yet all you people know is division and cannot function as one body as you should. Even my demonic realm can operate in unison without issue. Of course, the division of the human realm is encouraged by my kind through various campaigns of self-hate and outward hate, so an individual will either reject the image of God in which they were made or attempt to prove their image is the only image of God and all others are humans of a lower caste in God's eyes. This mindset causes groups to hinder one another from what *He* is calling each of them to do. This kind of hate and oppression is what keeps the heart of slavery, sexism, eugenics, racism, and bigotry beating strong, all the things my kind thrives on. Instead of healing the hate and oppression of something real in unification under God, my kind creates other categories of humanity that don't exist beyond delusion. These new categories claim long-standing persecution, causing the whole world to focus on them, ignoring the original division still thriving today, which has existed from the beginning of time. It's all about misdirection with this new method." Blight explains as he reaches out to adjust my tie, while the rest of me lay awkwardly on the cold floor.

"My kind learned that if you attack the social standing of an individual, making them enemy number one, you can control the change in that individual's ideals. People will do just about anything to get back in the good graces of the world, even if that means rejecting the basic principles of the Word of God. You're a perfect example of people who find a false sense of security in compromise. I'm still amazed by what your kind is willing to give up in exchange for the fleeting admiration of the world. As the Savior spoke in MK9 of the *Manual*, 'For whoever is ashamed of Me and My words in this adulterous and sinful generation, of him the Son of Man also will be ashamed when He comes in the glory of His Father with the holy angels.' Compromise like yours is the platform on which the Influencer Program was built. Church leaders across the globe are in fear of losing members through offending others by speaking the truth that some may not want to hear, so they instead choose to compromise. The leaders we control will only speak of supernatural blessings, God's love and how all people are *His* children; while ignoring the hard-hitting subjects they are afraid or ashamed to preach about. People like you will not teach about sin or conviction. They will not explain hell or repentance. They will not touch the tail end of RO1 in the *Manual*. For teachers like you, we work so that they will assure everyone that living any chosen lifestyle is okay with God and that all will meet again in Heaven. I mean it's not as if you will be bold and tell the truth? The truth can be offensive, as you mentioned earlier, especially if a person has built so many walls of self-delusion and pride around themselves to hide in their sins. We began coaxing pastors like you to teach the world that God has changed *His* mind about sin, and that what was once wicked or immoral is now, not so bad. What was once an abomination is now the norm and what *He* abhorred, *He's* now changed *His* mind on. Sad what one can believe in with a little coercion, isn't it?" Blight explains as he takes the wine bottle from my limp hand.

"The reason I'm telling you all of this is because you came here thinking that you could get a job here, in hell. You believed that there is a place of leadership in corruption here for you, and I find that just a bit *offensive* to my craft. The fact that you believed the so-called *work* you did on earth, would secure you a nice top-level placement here, as if you could compete in my world and do what we do here. I've had lifetimes of study and training, I was at the top of my graduating class, and you think that because you managed to deceive a few uneducated people and got all of … half a dozen of your congregation that has died so far to be added to our menu, that you deserve some sort of reward? You did what you did for your profit and esteem, not ours. In fact, even if you were more exceptional than any other human I've come across, you still would not be worthy of my kingdom. This place was not made for you, and yet you in all your pride and ego have the audacity to *choose* it, and why? Because you thought everything you accumulated on earth would follow you here? How many times did *He* reach out to you to turn it around? How many opportunities did *He* give you to seek *His* forgiveness and repent of your sins? More than my master, or me I'm sure. Yet you just kept pressing on and couldn't even taste the fruits of what you think you sowed. You only enjoyed the wine because it is a wonderful blend of your own sins and indiscretions." Blight holds the label up for me to see but I still struggle to read it as my vision cannot unjust to the dark kitchen.

"This is a wonderful concoction aptly named *Trespass*. Did you know this restaurant has enough supply from you that it's taken up most of the storage space in the cellar. We find it works best to marinate individuals from the inside out by getting them intoxicated on the wine of their own immoral and ungodly actions." Blight explains with a smile. Losing all my faculties now, I tip over and hit the cold tile floor. Blight leaves me there and begins to pluck lint off my suit, which is dark blue again. I cannot see them, but I am sure my watch and my phone are gone as there is no need for them anymore.

"Why are you doing this to me if I helped you all this time? I worked for you even when I didn't know it, it's not fair the way you're treating me now." I counter weakly as I use so much energy just to speak. Blight stares at me with a look of disgust.

"You still don't get it. I hate you and all of your kind with everything in me. If you were a good person, a righteous person, I'd still hate you, but at least I'd respect a righteous person for being a challenge. I've heard of people like you, but you're the first I've met that was so brazenly stupid. Ignoring or misinterpreting such chapters as RO6 in the *Manual*, you think heaven is about being a slave to God when the reality is *He* invited you into eternity as *His* child, and like any good child, *He* just wanted you to follow *Him.* What I find particularly funny is that your kind thinks to reject the *enslavement* of heaven means to accept the *freedom* of hell and I must ask, honestly, how free were you when I was dictating nearly everything you did? How free do you feel now? You were a slave to me on earth and could've been free in heaven but instead, you're here for all eternity." Blight replies.

"So what does that mean that I'm going to be a slave here in hell? Am I doomed to become one of these faceless bussers?" I manage to ask though it is exhausting to talk.

"I'm afraid not, we keep our slaves up top on earth. Down here you are needed only for one last thing, and that's sustenance." Blight replies as two bussers enter with a trolley car and two immobile, frightened looking diners stretched across the top. The bussers disappear behind the cooking station where the chef is preparing the next meal.

LEFTOVERS

8

"My biggest regret is that in this entire meeting I gained no solid, reliable insight on what to do about our little Ramona. I have a few ideas but I am doubting them already. Ever since she encountered *Him* I knew things were going downhill for me, and it only got worse after her baptism. She is just so hungry for the very Word you deprived her of and I've been trying so hard to derail her. I even led her to meet a young man that put her down all the time for her lack of education in the Word of God and for having a blasphemer and false prophet for a father. Contrary to the direction of RO14 of the *Manual*, the young man would berate her for what he considered her weakness in the faith and attempt to dispute everything. He believed that his church was the only one unto salvation and his Bible College the only one that taught it correctly. Like those of 1TY6:4 of the *Manual*, the young man prided himself on what he knew of the Word, which was absolutely nothing, and he loved to argue for the sake of arguing. You know the type; in fact, you *are* the type, especially when Ramona brought to your attention the corruption you were walking in and you insulted her and practically disowned her. However, *He* was there to encourage her to learn and she's very open to the wisdom *He* has been giving her. Not for profit like you, her

intentions are to help her family and to undo my work. If only she were unread like you this whole mission would've been accomplished a long time ago. I suppose it is my own fault for looking for a challenge." Blight says sourly. Three more trolleys piled with bodies come through the kitchen.

"I even tried to confuse her with thoughts about you and Jay and the rest of her family. It really hit home for Ramona that salvation is not just about getting yourself into heaven, it's about the people around you that you may or may not see there when the time comes. It's about the people who openly disobey God in a war of the flesh. The sinner may or may not care to justify their actions, even to the point of twisting the gospel to satisfy a false vindication as Ramona so often watched you and her siblings do. I tried to form in her one of two possible directions. When Ramona watched you and the rest of your family turn to sin, this made her question sin itself, instead of you all. So few people want to think that their unbelieving spouse, or their atheist parent, their hedonist child or their undecided agnostic best friend won't be joining them in heaven. In their own minds, many people question whether heaven is really that difficult or restrictive to get into to comfort themselves, while completely ignoring the narrowness of the gate in MW7 of the *Manual* as we discussed earlier. This idea is best in preventing the believer from praying for his or her own friends and family. Why should they if they believe some sins are really not very bad and in the end, God will just surprise them all by letting everyone into heaven? Lack of genuine prayer causes the sin to grow and spread unchecked, so that the perspective of the non-believer will eventually overwhelm and corrupt that of the believer. Then the other side of the approach is the believer attacking the non-believers and attempting to force salvation down their throats after losing all sense of love and compassion. This also works in my favor, as the believer can become careless and indifferent in their salvation while attempting to condemn others to hell. In this situation, I can go from one corrupted individual into two. The believer will eventually walk in hate and judgment toward unbelievers while thinking themselves the better of everyone else due to their misguided confidence in their own supposed righteousness. At the same time the unbeliever would now believe in God but believe *Him* to be one of hate and *His* children all elitist as *He* is misrepresented by the fallen believer, so trust me when I say, you could never do my job." Blight adds as a busser approaches with an empty cart but Blight raises a hand to stop him.

"It's alright, I'm not quite done with this one yet, so you can save him for last." Blight tells the busser who quickly exits to collect someone else.

"Where are they going to take me?" I ask as fear is finally setting in.

"Where all others like you end up, you vessels of wrath; like the man who sold his Savior for a few pieces of silver or the masses who chanted for the release of a murderer instead of the *One* who came to give them life. Like the leaders who had the most innocent *Man* in the world convicted on false chargers, and the Pharaoh of ancient Egypt whose heart was hardened on purpose to glorify God. In the end, even their sinful actions fulfilled *His* purposes and showed *His* power above all other things, much like your legacy on earth now. Damaging your reputation on earth only seemed to draw more individuals to the truth. Your daughter Ramona has proven to be the formidable foe you never were, reaching even her mother with love, compassion, patience, and forgiveness amidst the fallout of your sins and indiscretions even after nearly a decade. She does not agree with how your family lives, but how she loves them anyway; it is repulsive to me. I fear dissolution from service if I cannot turn this around, but then again I cannot contend with *Him* as *He* has stirred even Sasha's heart to pray with her little sister. That's not to say she's saved, but I fear with time there is opportunity, as Sasha is starting to question things and see a link between her depression and the relationships she's been guided into." Blight admits with a tone of regret.

"Then send me back and let me continue what *we* started. With me, you can win this. You can have my daughters, my entire family and more churchgoers for the price of me." I plead but Blight stands up straight and brushes the invisible dust off his pants.

"I'm afraid it only works that way in the movies Mr. Graves. People like you don't seem to grasp that the flesh you catered to and lived in on earth is long gone and rotting away. You didn't even get a funeral due to the shame of how you lived. As in RO9 of the *Manual, He* made his power known upon vessels of wrath like you, while showing the riches of *His* glory upon vessels of mercy like Ramona. You had your chance to change, but unlike Saul who became Paul and went from one of wrath to one of mercy after an encounter on a road, you disregarded every opportunity to turn it around and instead continued to do wrong, hoping it would turn out right for you. How I would have loved to taste even a tiny drop of that delicious unrighteousness in you but sadly you are reserved for the senior members of this kingdom and they are very hungry. I will take comfort in the fact that my master has allowed me to dine on my work so far through the members of your congregation whom I managed to corrupt onto death and, in the end, this assessment was not a total loss as I'm sure I'll be allowed to continue my work among your family or another. While this is the end of the line for you I will return to them at a more opportune time." Blight says and a busser returns for me. Someone lifts me onto the cart as if I weigh nothing at all.

"My God, please don't do this!" I beg, completely out of character but running out of options.

"Of course, now you call on *Him*. I'm more than happy to say it is too late, you worked injustice and corrupted God's Word for profit and *He* has already turned *His* face from you." Blight explains slowly as the cart begins to move away with me on it. "But fear not my friend, as heaven's doors are shut to you now, there is still a place for you here tonight as the main dish for the top leaders of this kingdom." Blight says as he holds a menu up to the light and I can just make out my signature. The wheels of the cart move slowly toward the chopping block and the chef whom I mocked for his lack of culinary skills. Blight walks slowly beside me deeper into the kitchen, his smile wide with satisfaction.

"Perhaps when you are served on a nice shiny platter, you will find that esteem among the demonic realm that you so desperately craved among humanity. Might I suggest now, that you enjoy it while it lasts, because if you haven't yet realized you are about to experience pain you never thought possible; and please don't believe that death will bring you peace because you are already dead. This is not your death, but the beginning of your eternal torment of being digested in the belly of hell. Here you will come to understand the definition of eternity in which you will have more than enough time to regret your life choices. It is a hard lesson warned in chapter MK8 of the *Manual*; that it profits a man absolutely nothing to gain the whole world at the cost of his own soul, and that fact does leave quite a bitter aftertaste." Blight adds as I descend deeper into the darkness of the eternal pit. A putrid smell of searing meat that could only be human flesh enters my nose as I can hear the chef's butcher knife sharpened in preparation of my arrival.

"Then they will cry to the *Lord,* but *He* will not hear them; *He* will even hide *His* face from them at that time, because they have been evil in their deeds."

- MICAH 3:4

ABOUT THE AUTHOR

Dawn Nicole Evans was born and raised in Southern California. She grew up a book lover and spent all her spare time in the library. While reading was one of her passions, a love for writing her own stories followed close behind.

It was not until her late twenties that Dawn found her way to church to hear the Word of God and it changed her life forever. Years later she would begin to dive into her calling of writing about the excellence of God and the good things in life that are sometimes harder to see.

Her focus is on encouraging others in different seasons of life to honor God and to know that God's Word is not invalid or outdated in any way, but may be more crucial now to our lives than ever before.